"THE game is in progress, Hannah, and the players on both sides know the score," Schellenberg said. "Isn't that your American phrase?"

"Is that how you see it? Just a game?"

"Of course it is—a great and terrible game that, once started, is impossible to stop. The game controls us; we don't control the game. It's like a fairground carousel. Once it's in motion, that's it."

"You could always try jumping off."

"Too late for that now. I'm trapped along with thousands like me. You think I believe that madman back there in Berlin?"

They stood there, confronting each other.

"Why?" she whispered, and there was pain in her voice. "I don't understand."

Schellenberg put a hand under her chin and smiled gently. "Life, my Hannah, has a habit on occasion of seizing one by the throat and refusing to let go." He kissed her gently on the mouth, turned, and walked away.

Fawcett Crest Books
by Harry Patterson:

THE VALHALLA EXCHANGE   23449 $2.25

TO CATCH A KING   24323 $2.95

TO CATCH
A KING

Harry
Patterson

FAWCETT CREST • NEW YORK

TO CATCH A KING

This book contains the complete text of the original hardcover edition.

Published by Fawcett Crest Books, a unit of CBS Publications, the Consumer Publishing Division of CBS Inc., by arrangement with Stein and Day Publishers

ISBN: 0-449-24323-0

Printed in the United States of America

First Fawcett Crest printing: November 1980

10 9 8 7 6 5 4 3 2 1

For my daughter SARAH,
from one unashamed romantic to another....

TO CATCH
A KING

PROLOGUE

IN JULY 1940, Walter Schellenberg, SS BrigadeFührer and Major General of Police, was ordered by Hitler to proceed to Lisbon to kidnap the Duke and Duchess of Windsor, then staying in a villa at Estoril after fleeing the German occupation of France. This story is an attempt to recreate events surrounding that astonishing episode. Most of it is documented historical fact although certain sections must obviously be a matter of conjecture. The person who emerges from the whole bizarre affair with the most credit is the Duke of Windsor himself. This book is a tribute to a gallant and honorable gentleman.

ONE

JUST AFTER midnight, it started to rain and the Portuguese policeman brought a cape from his sentry box and placed it around her shoulders without a word.

It was quite cold now and she walked a few paces along the road to keep warm, pausing to look back across the mouth of the Tagus to where the lights of Lisbon gleamed in the distance.

A long way; not as far as Berlin or Paris or Madrid, but she was here now, finally, outside the pink stucco villa at Estoril. The final end of things, more tired than she had ever been in her life before, and suddenly, she wanted it to be over.

11

She walked back to the policeman at the gate. "Please," she said in English. "How much longer? I've been here almost an hour."

Which was foolish because he didn't understand her. There was the sound of a car coming up the hill, headlights flashed across the mimosa bushes, and a black Mercedes braked to a halt a few yards away.

The man who got out of the rear was large and powerfully built. He was bareheaded and wore glasses, and his hands were pushed into the pockets of a dark mackintosh.

He said something briefly in Portuguese to the policeman, then turned to the girl. His English was quite excellent.

"Miss Winter, isn't it? Miss Hannah Winter?"

"Yes, that's right."

"Could I see your passport?"

She got it out quickly, her hands fumbling in the cold so that the cape slipped from her shoulders. He replaced it for her politely, then took the passport.

"So—an American citizen."

"Please," she said, a hand on his sleeve. "I must see the Duke. It's a matter of the gravest urgency."

He looked down at her calmly for a moment, then nodded to the policeman, who started to open the gate. The car rolled forward. He held the door for her. She climbed inside. He followed.

With a sudden burst of power, the Mercedes jumped forward, the driver swinging on the wheel, taking them around in a circle and back down the hill toward Lisbon.

She had been thrown into the corner and now he pulled her upright roughly and switched on the light. He was still clutching her passport.

"Hannah Winter—American citizen? I think not." He tore it apart and flung it into the corner. "Now this, I think, would be a much more accurate description."

The passport he pushed into her hands was German. She opened it in fascinated horror. The picture that stared out at her was her own.

"Fräulein Hannah Winter," he said, "Born in Berlin on November the ninth, nineteen-eighteen. Do you deny this?"

She closed the passport and pushed it back at him, fighting to control her panic. "My name is Hannah Winter but I am an American citizen. The American Embassy will confirm this."

"The Reich does not acknowledge the right of its citizens to change nationalities to suit their inclinations. You were born a German. I confidently predict you will die one."

The streets were deserted and they drove

very fast, so that already they were into the city and moving down toward the river.

He said, "An interesting city, Lisbon. To get into any foreign embassy it's necessary to pass through a Portuguese police checkpoint. So, if you'd tried to get into either the British or American Embassies, we would still have got you."

She said, "I don't understand. When I asked to be admitted the man on the gate said he'd have to check with headquarters."

"It's simple. The Portuguese police have accepted an extradition warrant to be served on Hannah Winter on a charge of murder—murder three times over. In fact, they've agreed to expedite the matter."

"But you—you're not the police."

"Oh, but we are. Not the Portuguese variety, but something rather more interesting." He was speaking in German now. "Sturmbannführer Kleiber of the Berlin office of the Gestapo. My colleague, Sturmscharführer Gunter Sindermann."

It was like something out of a nightmare, and yet the tiredness she felt was overwhelming so that nothing seemed to matter any more.

"What happens now?" she asked, dully.

Kleiber switched off the light so that they were in darkness again. "Oh, we'll take you home," he said. "Back to Berlin. Don't worry. We'll look after you."

His hand was on her knee, sliding up over the silk stocking to her thigh.

It was his biggest single mistake, for the disgust his actions engendered galvanized her into life again. She fumbled for the handle of the door, holding her breath as his hand moved higher. The Mercedes slowed to allow a water cart to pass. She shoved Kleiber away with all her strength, pushed open the door, and scrambled into the darkness, losing her balance, rolling over twice.

The shock effect was considerable, and when she got to her feet she had to lean against the wall for a moment. The Mercedes had pulled up farther along the street and started to reverse. She had lost one of her shoes, but there was nothing to be done about that. She kicked off the other, plunged into the nearest alley, and started to run.

A few moments later, she emerged on to the waterfront. It was still raining heavily and a considerable fog rolled in from the Tagus and street lamps were few and far between. There seemed to be no shops, no houses, simply tall gaunt warehouses rising into the night.

As the fog closed in around her, it was as if she was the only person in the world, and then she heard the sound of her pursuers echoing between the walls of the alley behind her.

She started to run again, lightly in stockinged feet. She was cold—very cold—and then a light appeared dimly in the fog on the other side of the street backing onto the river. A red neon sign said *Joe Jackson's* and underneath *American Bar*.

She hurried across, filled with desperate hope, but there was no light inside and the glass doors were locked. She rattled them furiously in helpless rage. There was a wharf at the side of the building, another door with a light above it marked *Stage*. She tried that too, hammering on it with her fists, and then Kleiber ran around the corner, a Luger in his left hand.

"I'll teach you," he said softly. "Little Jewish bitch."

As Sindermann arrived she turned and ran along the wharf into the fog.

Joe Jackson had dark, wavy hair, pale face, hazel-green eyes, and a slight, ironic quirk that seemed to permanently lift the corner of his mouth. The weary, detached smile of a man who had found life more corrupt than he had hoped.

He always closed Mondays. For one thing, it gave everyone a night off and for another, there was little trade to be had at the beginning of the week. It gave him a chance at the books in peace and quiet, which was what he was doing when Hannah first rattled the front door.

A drunk, he thought, looking for another drink, and returned to his accounts. A moment later, he heard her at the side door. He was aware of a murmur of voices and then a sharp cry. He opened the right-hand drawer of the desk and took out a Browning automatic, got to his feet, and moved out of the office quickly.

He was wearing a navy blue sweater, dark slacks. A small man, no more than five feet five or six, with good shoulders.

He unlocked the stage door and stood, listening. There was a choked cry from farther along the wharf. He went forward, taking his time, silent on rope-soled sandals.

There was a lamp on a pole at the end of the wharf. In its light, he saw Hannah Winter on her back. Sindermann crouched over her body. Kleiber stood above them, still holding the Luger.

"And now, Miss Winter," he said in English. "A lesson in manners."

"I don't think so," Jackson called softly.

He shot Kleiber in the left forearm, driving him back against the rail, the Luger jumping into the dark waters below.

Kleiber made no sound—simply stood there, gripping his arm, waiting for what was to come.

Hannah Winter, still pinned beneath Sindermann's weight, gazed up at Jackson blankly. He tapped the German on the back of the head with the barrel of the Browning.

Sindermann stood up and raised his hands. There was no fear on his face, simply a sullen rage. Jackson helped the girl to her feet. For the briefest of moments his attention was diverted as she sagged against him. Sindermann charged, head down.

Jackson swung the girl to one side and stuck out a foot. Sindermann tripped and continued headfirst over the rail. They could hear him floundering about in the water below.

Jackson had an arm about her again. "You all right?"

"I am now," she said.

He gestured with the Browning at Kleiber, who stood waiting, blood oozing between his fingers. "What about this one?"

"Let him go."

"No police?"

"It's not a police matter," she said wearily.

Jackson nodded to Kleiber. "You heard the lady."

The German turned and walked away rapidly. Jackson pushed the Browning in his belt at the small of his back and picked her up in both arms.

"Okay, angel, let's get you inside."

She stood under the hot shower for twenty minutes before toweling herself dry and putting on the robe he'd given her. The apartment was on the third floor at the rear of the club and overlooked the river. It was neat and functional and sparingly furnished, with little evidence of any belongings of real personal worth. The present resting place of a man who had kept on the move for most of his life.

The sliding windows stood open and she found him standing on the broad wooden veranda, a drink in one hand, looking out over the river. A foghorn sounded somewhere in the distance as a ship moved out to sea.

She shivered. "The loneliest sound in the world."

"Trains," he said gravely. "According to Thomas Wolfe. But let me get you a cognac. You look as if you could do with it."

His voice was good Boston American. "Where are you from?" she asked.

"Cape Cod. Fishing village called Wilton. A long, long time ago." He handed her the cognac. "And you?"

"New York, although it's a matter of dispute

in some quarters," she said and sipped a little of the cognac.

He lit a cigarette. "Those friends of yours out there? You said it wasn't police business."

"True," she said. "You see, they are police. A variety peculiar to the Third Reich, known as the Gestapo."

He was no longer smiling now. He closed the window and turned to face her.

"You're Joe Jackson, aren't you?"

"That's right, but we've never met."

"No," she said. "But I know all about you. My name is Hannah Winter. I'm a singer. Born in Berlin, but my parents took me to America when I was two years old. I returned to Berlin to sing at my uncle Max's club two months ago. You know a piano player called Connie Jones?"

Jackson smiled. "I certainly do. He's in Madrid at the Flamenco with his trio right now. Due to appear here next week."

"A fortnight ago, he was backing me at my uncle's place in Berlin. The Garden Room. He was the one who told me about the great Joe Jackson who runs the best American bar in Lisbon. Who fought with the International Brigade in Spain and flew fighters against the Nazi Condor Legion."

Jackson said, "All right. I'll buy it."

She said, "Have you ever heard of a man called Dr. Ricardo de Espirito Santo é Silva?"

"Portuguese banker. Has a villa at Estoril."

"Would you happen to know who his house guests are at the moment?"

"Common knowledge. The Duke and Duchess of Windsor."

"But not for much longer," she said. "Not if the Nazis have anything to do with it." She started to shake.

"Okay," Joe Jackson held her arms for a moment, then drew her down on the couch beside him in front of the fire.

"Now calm down. Just take your time and tell me about it—everything there is to tell."

TWO

IT BEGAN, if it began anywhere at all, with a man called Erich von Mannstein, who at the beginning of 1940 was chief of staff to General Gerd von Rundstedt.

Von Mannstein, who was to become the most brilliant commander in the field that the German Army produced during the Second World War, was a superb tactician who constantly challenged the views of his superiors, particularly their plans to invade France and the Low Countries.

Faced with demotion, his career threatened, chance took him to a dinner party given by Adolf Hitler on the 17th of February, 1940. At that meeting he took the opportunity of outlining to the Führer his own alternative plan, an audacious drive to the Channel by Panzers through the Ardennes, aimed at separating the British and French armies.

Hitler became so obsessed with the idea that, in time, he came to believe that it was his own. On the 10th of May, it was put into action with incredible effect. Within a matter of days, the Allied armies were in a headlong retreat.

By the 2nd of June, thanks to Hitler's decision to halt his Panzers on the Aa Canal, most of the British Expeditionary Force managed to escape from the beaches of Dunkirk. On the afternoon of the 22nd, the French signed an armistice document in the forest of Compiègne in the old wooden dining car in which Marshal Foch had dictated terms to the Germans in November, 1918.

Early the following morning, Hitler, accompanied by Keitel and a few hand-picked companions, landed at the Le Bourget airport and was driven into Paris. The most devastating campaign in modern warfare was over.

In the chaos that was the rest of France, particularly in the south, the roads were crowded with refugees pushing desperately for the Pyrenees and the Spanish border, many of them

British citizens who had lived on the Riviera for years.

Among them was a convoy of cars headed by a Buick towing a loaded trailer. At a small town west of Arles, a barricade had been erected by gendarmes to prevent any further passage to refugees.

As the Buick slowed to a halt, the small, rather slight-looking man seated beside the dark-haired woman in the back, stood up so that he could be clearly seen. He smiled with considerable charm, but the authority there was unmistakable.

"I am the Prince of Wales," he said in excellent French. "Let me pass, if you please."

The statement was not strictly accurate, but to millions of Europeans it was the title by which they still remembered him. The officer in charge gazed at him in astonished recognition, then saluted and barked a quick order to his men. The barricades were hastily removed and the Duke and Duchess of Windsor and their party passed through.

In Berlin on the following Friday it was raining as Hannah Winter left her apartment in Köenigstrasse. It was eight-thirty, an hour before the first cabaret of the evening at the Garden Room, which was a good mile away near

the Unter den Linden. Not much chance of a
taxi these days so she'd have to hurry. There
was a Mercedes parked across the street. She
glanced at it hopefully, then realized it was a
private car and started to walk.

Two young men came around the corner and
moved toward her. They were in Nazi Party
uniform of some sort, although what it signified
she had no idea. There were so many uniforms
these days. They paused, blocking the pavement, the faces beneath the peaked caps hard
and cruel, ripe for mischief. She was in trouble
and knew it.

"Papers," one of them said.

She remembered Uncle Max's first rule:
Never show fear. "I'm an American citizen," she
replied calmly.

"So?" He snapped his fingers. She produced
her passport from her bag and handed it over.

"Hannah Winter—twenty-two. That's a good
age." His companion sniggered and he returned
the passport. "And your pass."

The other one moved closer, enjoying this, his
eyes stripping her. She took out her pass reluctantly and handed it over.

He laughed delightedly. "Well, would you
look at this. A Yid." He moved closer. "Where's
your star, Jew? You know it's a serious offense

to be out without it. We're going to have to do something about that."

He was very close to her now, forcing her back toward the mouth of the alley behind. There was the sound of a car door slamming and she saw a man emerge from the rear of the Mercedes and start across the street.

"That's enough," he called softly through the rain.

He was of medium height, wore a slouch hat and a black leather coat. A cigarette dangled from the left-hand corner of his mouth.

Her interrogator scowled ferociously. "Clear off, if you know what's good for you. This is police business."

"Is that so?" the man said calmly. "Fräulein Winter, is that right? My name is Schellenberg. I heard the exchange sitting in my car over there. Are these men annoying you?"

"She's a Yid, out on the street without her Star of David."

"And an American citizen, if I heard correctly. Is this not so, Fräulein?"

His smile had a kind of ruthless charm that was accentuated by the dueling scar on one cheek, and her stomach was, for some unaccountable reason, hollow with excitement.

"Yes," she said.

A hand grabbed Schellenberg's arm and

shook him furiously. "Clear off—now. Unless you want your face kicked in."

Schellenberg wasn't in the least put out. "Oh dear, you are a nasty little boy, aren't you?"

He waved his right hand casually. Two men in uniform as black as the Mercedes got out of the car and hurried across. Their cuff-titles carried the legend *RFSS* picked out in silver thread: *Reichsführer der SS* the cuff-title of Himmler's personal staff.

Schellenberg said, "A lesson is needed here, I think." He took the girl by the arm. "Fräulein."

As he guided her firmly across the road toward the car, there was the sound of a blow, a cry of pain, but she did not look back.

It was fifteen minutes later when the Mercedes pulled in to the curb in front of the Garden Room. Hans, the doorman, came forward hesitantly, a look of astonishment on his face when he saw who was inside. He opened the door and Schellenberg got out and turned to assist her.

"So, this is where you work?" He examined the photographs in the glass case beneath the poster. "'Hannah Winter and the Connie Jones trio, direct from the Albany Club, New York.' Sounds interesting. I must come one night."

She said calmly, "I'm Jewish, as you very well know, and as you can see from the photo, Connie is a Negro. I hardly think we'd be of much interest to a member of the master race."

He smiled gently. '"Shall we go in?"

"I use the stage door."

"And I, on the contrary, always go in by the front."

He had her by the arm again and she went without protest. Hans hurriedly got the door open for them. Her uncle was at the front desk talking to the hat check girl. He was a shrewd, kindly-looking man, with a shock of gray hair and steel-rimmed glasses, who always managed to appear untidy in spite of his dinner jacket.

At the sight of his niece and Schellenberg, the smile was wiped instantly from his face and he hurried forward.

"Hannah, my love, what's happened? You are in trouble?"

"I was, but not any more, thanks to Herr Schellenberg. This is my uncle, Max Winter."

"Herr Winter," Schellenberg said amiably and turned back to Hannah.

She was at that time just twenty-two, a small, rather hippy girl with good legs; a face that was handsome rather than beautiful, with high cheekbones, dark eyes, and black hair worn unfashionably long.

He took her right hand, holding it for a mo-

ment. "And now, Fräulein, after seeing you in
a better light, I am more determined than ever
to catch your act—isn't that the American
phrase? But not tonight, I regret to say."

He raised her hand to his lips, and again she
was conscious of that unwanted hollow excitement.

"Herr Winter."

He went out, and when Hannah glanced at
her uncle she found that he had turned quite
pale. "Uncle Max—what is it?"

"That man," he whispered. "Where did you
meet him? Don't you know who he is? That is
Walter Schellenberg, SS Brigadeführer and
Major General of Police. Heydrich's right-hand
man."

Hannah Winter had been born in November,
1918, two days before the Armistice was signed
to end that most terrible of all wars. Her father,
Simon, once a violinist with the Berlin Phil-
harmonic, emigrated to New York in 1920 and
opened a small restaurant on Forty-second
Street in partnership with his wife's father.
During the years of Prohibition, the establishment developed into a highly successful night
club, but his health had never been good because of chest wounds received while serving

as an infantryman on the Somme, and he died in July, 1929.

The club, after Prohibition, once again became a restaurant and prospered under the shrewd direction of his wife. Hannah she had raised to be a nice Jewish girl who would one day make a good marriage, have kids, do all the right things.

It might have worked, except for one important point. Hannah Winter had been blessed with an extraordinary singing voice. She discovered her talent by chance, singing with a student jazz band at high school. From that time on, she had never seriously contemplated any other way of life.

At seventeen, she had appeared at the Paloma Ballroom in Hollywood with Benny Goodman. As a straight band singer she had toured with Artie Shaw and Tommy Dorsey.

But she was at her best always in the more enclosed world of club and cabaret, preferably backed by a good trio. It was then that she was able to bring an intensity to her performance of the average popular song that perhaps rivaled anything Bessie Smith had been able to do with the blues.

And she could have been at the Paramount Studios in Hollywood now doing a film with Bing Crosby if it hadn't been for Uncle Max, her father's younger brother, who, in spite of the fact that he had been a naturalized American citizen for twenty-five years, had horrified them all by returning to the city of his birth in 1937 to open a night club.

Which was why Hannah was here. To persuade him that it was time to get out. But events had overtaken her with frightening rapidity. The Phony War was over and the Nazis were poised on the Channel coast, with England next stop and nothing standing in the way.

She was applying her make-up when there was a knock at the door and her uncle entered. He pulled a chair forward and lit one of the small cigars he favored, watching her in the mirror.

"All right—what happened?"

She told him quickly, continuing the work on her face, then went behind the screen to change.

"Not good," he said. "Perhaps it would be as well if I explained a few things to you. In Germany today the SS is all-powerful, but within the organization they have their own secret service department—the SD. Heydrich is Director General, although still under the authority of Himmler."

"And Schellenberg?"

"He's in charge of the counterespionage sec-

tion, but more important, he's Heydrich's favorite. His right-hand man." She made no reply
as she slid a long black dress over her head,
taking care not to spoil her make-up. "Do you
understand any of this?"

"Not really," she said, emerging from behind
the screen and turning so that he could button
up the back of the dress. "So many titles—so
many names. It's all very confusing. And the
uniforms—every second person you meet seems
to have one."

He took her hand. "This isn't Forty-second
Street, Hannah."

She sat down facing him. "All right, Uncle
Max. Then let's go home."

"You are," he said. "All arranged—tickets
and everything."

"I don't understand?"

"Connie and the boys leave Monday morning
by train for Paris. The same night they've got
berths on the sleeper to Madrid, and so have
you."

"And when was all this decided?"

"Today. The boys have got a week at the Flamenco Club in Madrid. You knew that."

"But I haven't."

"No, but you can carry straight on to Lisbon
from there. Plenty of boats going to New York.
You might even get a seat on the Clipper."

"And you?"

"I've got things to do here."

"Then I'm not going."

"Oh, yes, you are, Liebchen." She had never heard quite that tone in his voice before. He patted her hand and got up. "We've got a lot in tonight. I'd better go and see how the food's working out."

As he reached the door she said, "Uncle Max, you're mixed up in something, aren't you? Something serious?"

He smiled gently. "I'll see you later. Slay the people, Liebchen."

The door closed softly behind him and she sat there, staring into the mirror, her mind in turmoil. A moment later, there was another knock and Connie Jones glanced in.

"Are you ready?"

She managed a smile. "As much as I ever will be."

Connie was a large, rugged-looking Negro of forty-five with close-cropped graying hair. Born and raised in New Orleans, he had been playing the piano like a dream since the age of seven and couldn't read a note of music.

"Trouble?" he asked, sitting on the edge of her dressing table.

"Uncle Max tells me I leave with you on Monday."

"That's it. Twelve hours to gay Paree, then the night express to Madrid from Austerlitz Station, and I can't shake the dust of this town soon enough." He lit a cigarette. "You're worried about the old man, aren't you?"

"He says he isn't coming, Connie, but if he stays here . . ."

"If ever a man knew what he was doing, it's your Uncle Max, kid. I'd leave it to him." He took her hand. "You worry too much and that ain't good because we got a show to do, so let's get with it."

She took a deep breath, stood up, and followed him out, immediately aware of the club noises. People talking, the laughter, the hustle. It had an electricity to it that never failed in its effect on her.

Two other Negroes waited in the shadows beside the small stage, both younger than Connie: Billy Joe Halc, the bass player, and Harry Gray, the drummer. They dumped their cigarettes and moved onstage with Connie.

Hannah waited, and then the spots bathed the stage in white light and Uncle Max's voice boomed from somewhere at the rear of the room. "And now, the Garden Room proudly presents, direct from New York, the one and only Hannah Winter!"

And as Connie and the boys moved into a

solid driving arrangement of "St. Louis Blues," she walked onstage to thunderous applause and started to sing her heart out.

Reinhard Heydrich, unlike most Nazi party members, had been born a gentleman. Cashiered from the Navy, he had joined the SS and had been quickly chosen by Himmler as his deputy. His rise to the position of Head of the Reich Main Security Office, one of the most powerful positions in the state, was a tribute as much to his total lack of any kind of humanity as to his qualities of leadership and superior intelligence.

When Schellenberg entered he was seated at his desk in his Prinz Albrechtstrasse office and was wearing the full dress uniform of an SS Obergruppenführer, for he had just returned from dining with Hitler at the Reich Chancellery.

"Ah, there you are, Walter," he said amiably. "You've been having a busy evening, I hear, playing Galahad to the Winter girl."

"Is there anything you don't know?" Schellenberg said. "It's only just happened, for God's sake."

"One survives, Walter, in this wicked old world of ours by knowing everything there is to know about everything and everybody."

"Which in this case would seem to mean that the people who work for me report to you first."

"Of course," Heydrich smiled. "Tell me about her. How long has she been under surveillance?"

"Since she arrived. Two months now."

"And she really fell for this little drama of yours tonight?"

"I think so."

"What exactly do you hope to achieve? Access to her bed or information?"

"It's her uncle we're after, remember," Schellenberg said. "The fact that he's an American citizen makes things difficult."

"But he was born a German," Heydrich said impatiently. "I've seen his file, and the Führer has stated often enough that citizens of the Reich do not have the right to change nationality."

"The Americans might have a different viewpoint on that one," Schellenberg pointed out. "And this is hardly the moment to antagonize Washington."

"So—are we any further forward with this Winter affair?"

"Not really. As you can see from his file, he attended the University of Berlin as a youth and was a member of the Communist Party. It is my belief that he still is."

"A Soviet agent possibly?"

"Perhaps. Certainly involved with the Socialist Underground and probably also the illegal transfer of Jews from the Reich."

"Then what are you waiting for? Arrest him."

"Not just yet," Schellenberg said. "If we wait a little longer we get not only Winter, but his entire organization. And he is under surveillance at all hours."

Heydrich sat there frowning, then nodded. "Very well, Walter. You can have another week. Seven days and then..." He stood up. "What are you going to do now?"

Schellenberg knew what was coming. "Go home to bed."

"Nonsense," Heydrich grinned. "The night's still young. We'll make the rounds of a few nightclubs. Help yourself to a drink while I change."

He went out and Schellenberg sighed, moved to the drinks cabinet, and poured himself a Scotch.

He had been born in Saarbrücken in 1910, the son of a piano maker. Cultured and intelligent by nature and with a gift for languages, he had entered the University of Bonn at the age of nineteen in the faculty of medicine, but changed to the study of law after two years.

Well qualified, but penniless, he saw oppor-

tunity in the rise of the Nazi Party in 1933 and
accepted the suggestion of one of his professors
that he join the SS. His gift for languages
brought him to the attention of Heydrich, who
had recruited him at once into the SD, where
his rise had been rapid.

A number of successful intelligence opera-
tions had combined to consolidate his position,
culminating in the Venlo incident in 1939, during which he had posed as a resistance agent
to gain the confidence of three British MI-5
agents in Holland. This had led to their kid-
napping by SS troops on neutral territory.

Decorated by the Führer himself, he had been
promoted SS Brigadeführer and Major General
of Police and was still only thirty years of
age.

Of course, he had his enemies, but Heydrich
and his wife liked him, so that he moved socially
in the very best circles in Berlin. But there was
a price to pay, including the occasional night
out with Heydrich, whose sexual appetite was
insatiable and who was never happier than
roaming the cabarets and clubs of the
Kurfürstendamm and Alexanderplatz.

Greatest irony of all, of course, was that Walter Schellenberg did not consider himself a
Nazi. Heydrich, Himmler, even the Führer, all
came to trust his judgment implicitly on intel-

ligence matters, and yet always in his mind he
stood on one side, a spectator of the whole sorry
charade, contemptuous as much of himself as
of them.

The rain beat against the window and he
raised his glass to his reflection, in mock salute.

THREE

ON THURSDAY morning just before noon, Schellenberg was working in his Prinz Albrechtstrasse office when the phone rang. He recognized the voice at once—von Ribbentrop.

"Schellenberg, are you free? I'd like you to come over to see me at once."

"Anything special?" Schellenberg asked the Foreign Minister.

"A matter of the utmost importance to the Reich. I can't discuss it on the phone."

Schellenberg called Heydrich at once and reported the situation, always aware of Heydrich's rage at even the slightest suggestion of his personal authority being usurped. For

once, Heydrich was more intrigued than anything else and told him to get on with it—with
the promise of a detailed report later.

Ribbentrop received Schellenberg in his private office at the Reich Chancellery.

"Good of you to come, my dear fellow. Sit
down and I'll get straight to the point. I am
speaking to you on behalf of the Führer himself
on this matter, by the way, so we are talking
of something with the highest security rating."

Schellenberg was immediately intrigued. "I
see. Please continue."

"Did you by any chance meet the Duke of
Windsor during his German tour in nineteen
thirty-seven?"

"No, I didn't have that pleasure."

"What is your personal opinion about the way
in which the English dealt with the crisis surrounding his abdication?"

"It seems to me they handled the whole problem very sensibly. Tradition and responsibility
had to take precedence over personal emotions."
Schellenberg shrugged. "I don't really see how
the British government could have acted any
differently."

Ribbentrop looked extremely put out. "I can
see this is one matter about which you have
been completely misinformed. The real reasons

behind the pressure for the Duke to abdicate were political. He was too socially aware; too determined to change the decadent English society into something forceful and forward-looking. Something more suited to modern needs."

"I see," Schellenberg said dryly. "He told you this?"

Ribbentrop didn't seem to hear him. "He was much impressed with everything he saw in Germany. The Führer received him at Berchtesgaden. They talked together for an hour."

He paused at the window. "At the moment the Führer is totally immersed in the planning of Operation Sea Lion—the invasion of England—which is why he asked me to handle this most important matter for him."

"I see."

"The Duke, as you know, was serving as a major general with Allied forces in France. During the debacle that followed our magnificent victory, he and the Duchess, with a few friends, managed to cross into Spain. They were in Madrid until recently. In fact the attitude of the Spaniards in the matter may be best summed up by this telegram I received from our Madrid ambassador, Von Stohrer. I have a copy here."

He passed it across and Schellenberg scanned it quickly.

> The Spanish Foreign Minister requests advice with regard to the treatment of the Duke and Duchess of Windsor who were to arrive in Madrid today, apparently in order to return to England by way of Lisbon. They assume we may be interested in detaining the Duke here and possibly in establishing contact with him.

Schellenberg handed the paper back. "I don't understand?"

"It's really very simple. The English are racially a part of our Germanic brotherhood. The Führer has no wish to destroy them. They could have an important part to play in the greater European ideal. He is convinced that any day now, the British Government will see this and will sue for peace. After all, they don't have much choice. They're finished."

"There's still the Channel to cross," Schellenberg pointed out.

"But there won't be any need, don't you see? And once a peace treaty has been concluded, there would be the question of the throne to consider. Much better for all concerned to see it occupied by a man loved by his people, who was also a good friend to Germany."

. It was with difficulty that Schellenberg stopped himself from laughing out loud. "Are you really serious, Minister?"

Ribbentrop seemed mildly surprised. "But of course. I have here a copy of a report sent to the American Secretary of State on the second of July by their Ambassador in Madrid in which he states that in a conversation with a member of the Embassy staff, the Duke declared that the most important thing now was to end the war before thousands more were killed or maimed to save the faces of a few politicians."

"Which hardly makes him a National Socialist," Schellenberg said.

Ribbentrop rolled on relentlessly. "The Duke and Duchess arrived in Lisbon recently and are staying at Estoril in the villa of a Portuguese banker, Dr. Ricardo de Espirito Santo é Silva. On their arrival they found two British flying boats waiting to take them to England. The Duke sent them back. Refused to go. Don't you find that interesting?"

"Did he give a reason?"

"According to our information, he insisted on the offer of a worthwhile post and assurances that the Duchess would be treated in future in full accord with her status as his wife."

"That seems reasonable," Schellenberg said. "They've hardly made the best use of his talents so far in this war. Has he had a reply?"

"Apparently Churchill is offering him the governorship of the Bahamas."

"Clever," Schellenberg said, "and practical. Three thousand miles from the war. Has he accepted?"

"Not yet. Quite obviously, he's stalling for time. We feel he would probably far rather stay on in Spain or possibly even in Switzerland. Naturally that gangster Churchill and his clique wouldn't like this, and we may assume that the British Secret Service would take a hand."

"In what way?"

"Oh, I should imagine the obvious ploy would be to make sure the Duke got on the boat to the Bahamas whether he wanted to or not, which is where you come in, Schellenberg. The Führer feels you would be the ideal man to speak to the Duke on our behalf. Offer any assistance he may need. Financial, for example, if that is necessary. Whatever happens, the Duke must be given help to reach the country of his choice."

"Even if that proves to be the Bahamas?"

Ribbentrop glanced at him. "My dear Schellenberg, as I've told you before on many occasions, that facetiousness of yours could well be the death of you one of these days."

"My apologies, Minister."

"To continue. If the Duke should prove in any way hesitant the Führer would have no objection to your helping him reach the right decision."

"By force?"

"If necessary. Naturally, it will also be your responsibility to see that the Duke and his wife are not exposed to any personal danger. A hunting trip into Spain is all it takes. Once you have them over the border, the rest is simple."

Schellenberg said, "And this is a direct order from the Führer himself?"

"But of course." Ribbentrop passed an envelope across. "You'll find everything you need in there. Total authority. I can only wish you well and envy your inevitable success in this matter."

Heydrich sat by the window in his office holding the document in his hand.

FROM THE LEADER AND CHANCELLOR OF
THE STATE
MOST SECRET

General Schellenberg is acting under

my direct and personal orders in a matter of the utmost importance to the Reich. He is answerable only to me. All personnel, military and civil, without distinction of rank, will assist him in any way he sees fit.

Adolf Hitler

"Nonsense!" Heydrich said. "Sheer bloody nonsense and all built on totally false assumptions."

There was a knock on the door and a young secretary entered with a file which she placed on his desk. She went out without a word and Heydrich tapped it with a finger.

"In here, Walter, is everything you need to know about the Duke of Windsor—everything recorded about him. But what have I taught you to be the first and most fundamental principle of intelligence work?"

"As the Jesuits put it, by the small things shalt thou know them."

"Exactly. It is not what a man says or what people say about him that is the truth. It is how he behaves, for character is action." He tapped the file. "And nowhere more so than with this

man. How would you describe him—in the
world's eyes?"

"A contradiction. Concerned about his fellow
men—his attitude to the English working classes
proved that—and yet fond of luxury and pleasure. A difficult man; reserved."

"Perhaps. Certainly stubborn."

"Because of his stand on the question of mar-
rying the Duchess? Some people might find that
admirable. In the past, the hypocrisy of many
kings of England in sexual matters is a fact
of history. Perhaps the Duke was actually taking a moral stance on this occasion as a matter
of principle. To do otherwise, to humiliate
the woman he loved might have seemed to him
the most contemptible thing he could imagine."

"When he was serving with the British Military Mission in France in what was meant to
be a dead-end job, he managed to make several
tours of the Maginot Line." Heydrich opened
the file. "There is a copy here of a letter sent
to the War Office by Major General Vyse. He
gives details of a report by the Duke after an
inspection of the French First Army and sum-
marizes it as follows:

    a.   There is little attempt at con-
           cealment.

b. The revetment of the antitank
    ditches is weak. Other antitank
    obstacles do not seem to be ade-
    quate.

c. Wiring against infantry, coin-
    cides on location with antitank
    obstacles so that the same bom-
    bardment would destroy both.

d. Antitank crews seem insuffi-
    ciently trained.

e. Work does not seem to be carried
    out intensively and very few
    troops were seen.

"You see?" Heydrich said. "Every evidence of
a first-class military mind. Anyway, take it
away. Go through the whole file. Get to know
the man and then at least you'll know what
you're talking about."

"You wish me to take on this task?"

"I'm not certain. I'll let you know this evening. In the meantime, do me the usual de-
partmental report. Everything Ribbentrop said.
I want it all down on paper."

When Schellenberg reached his own office he
called in Frau Huber, Heydrich's confidential
secretary. She was thirty-eight, a sensual,

rather fleshy-looking woman with no make-up, her hair pulled back from her face in a tight bun. She was a war widow already; her husband, a Sturmscharführer in the Leibstandarts SS Division, had been killed during the French campaign. In her simple white blouse and skirt, she was surprisingly attractive.

Schellenberg quickly dictated an account of his meeting with Ribbentrop. "As soon as possible, please."

She went out and he opened the Windsor file and started to work his way through it. It didn't take long, just under half an hour. As he finished, Frau Huber returned with the completed report. He checked it over and signed it.

"The usual copies?" she asked.

"Yes, one for the Reichsführer, one for me, and one for the file."

She went out. He sat there frowning for a moment, then picked up the phone and asked for Admiral Canaris at Abwehr Headquarters on the Tirpitz Ufer.

The Admiral, it seemed, was not available. Schellenberg smiled. That probably meant that, as it was Thursday afternoon, Canaris would be riding in the Tiergarten. He picked up the telephone, ordered a car, and left quickly.

When Frau Huber went into the copying

room, there was only a middle-aged woman on duty who was unfamiliar to her.

"Who are you?" she demanded.

"Irene Neumann. I usually work in Central Office."

"I see. Run this through the machine now. Three copies. One for the boss, one for General Schellenberg, and one for me. I'll wait."

The other woman set the machine up quickly. *For your eyes only—most secret.* She took in that much and then the phrase *Duke of Windsor* seemed to jump right out at her.

Frau Huber lit a cigarette and paced about the room restlessly. "Hurry up, for God's sake."

As the machine started, the phone rang in her office and she hurried to answer it. It was a routine matter taking only three or four minutes to handle. As she finished writing a memo, there was a nervous cough and she turned and found Irene Neumann standing there.

"Three copies, you said, Frau Huber?"

"All right. Put them on the desk."

The other woman did as she was told and went out. Back in the copying room she closed the door carefully, then opened a drawer and took out the extra copy of the Windsor report that she had made. She folded it carefully, raised her skirt, and slipped it inside the top of her stocking.

A moment later, the door opened and a young woman in SS Auxiliary uniform entered. "Have you been busy?"

"Not particularly."

"Good. You can go now."

She started to unbutton her uniform jacket and Irene Neumann took down her coat from behind the door and left.

Admiral Wilhelm Canaris was fifty-two. A U-boat commander of distinction during the First World War, he was now head of the Abwehr, the Intelligence Department of the German Armed Forces High Command. Although a loyal German, like many of the officer class, he loathed most aspects of the Nazi regime, an attitude that was to lead to his downfall and execution toward the end of the war.

Schellenberg was on close personal terms with him and they frequently rode together in the Tiergarten. As he waited beside his car, he could see the Admiral now, cantering along the ride between the trees followed by his two favorite dachshunds, who were obviously experiencing some difficulty in keeping up with him. He saw Schellenberg when still some little distance away, waved, and turned toward him.

He reined in and dismounted. "Business, Walter, or conversation?"

"Interchangeable, I usually find." Schellenberg called to his driver, "Come and hold the
Herr Admiral's horse."

They walked among the trees, the dachshunds waddling at their heels.

"How goes the war then, Walter? From your
point of view, of course."

"Well, Herr Admiral, I think we could agree
on that."

"And Sea Lion?"

"Only the Führer has the facts there."

"And expects the British to sue for peace any
day. Do you think they will?"

"Not really."

"Neither do I. Not with the Channel to cross.
And they always do so damned well with their
backs to the wall. You heard the gist of Churchill's speech? Fight on the beaches, in the
streets. Blood, sweat, tears."

"There's still the Luftwaffe to come."

"I know," Canaris said scornfully. "Fat Her-
mann boasting again. Reduce London to ashes,
bomb them into submission. Wasn't that what
he was supposed to do to the British Army at
Dunkirk? Instead, the Luftwaffe got all hell
knocked out of it by a handful of Spitfires."

His face was stiff with anger, and Schellenberg watched him closely. He genuinely liked
Canaris; admired him as a man. On the other

hand, the Admiral was undoubtedly indiscreet. He was already suspected by Heydrich and Himmler, as Schellenberg well knew, of having leaked the date of the attack in the West to the Allies, which if it was true, had certainly done them little good.

"Well, what is it, Walter? What do you wish to discuss? I know that devious mind of yours by now. Spit it out."

"I was wondering," Schellenberg said, "whether you had an opinion on the Duke of Windsor."

Canaris roared with laughter. "Has Ribbentrop dropped that one in your lap? My God, he really does have it in for you, doesn't he?"

"You know all about it then?"

"Of course I do. He approached me yesterday. He knows we have an organization in Lisbon. He seemed to think we could handle the whole affair."

"And why don't you?"

"Our man there is a German industrialist who operates under the cover of a flourishing import-export business. In Abwehr files he is called A-1416."

"Yes, I met him when I was last in Lisbon."

"The British Secret Service know him, I believe, as Hamlet."

"A double agent? Then why don't you have him eliminated?"

"Because he serves my purposes. Feeds them the kind of information I want them to have on occasion. It's a we-know-that-you-know-that-we-know-that-you-know situation. Needless to say I couldn't possibly give him the Windsor affair. He'd put the British straight onto it."

"And is that your only reason?"

"No—I think the whole thing a nonsense. A number of incidents concerning the Duke have been hopelessly misconstrued. To give you an example: a speech he made some years ago at a British Legion Rally suggesting that the time had come for British veterans of the First World War to hold out the hand of comradeship to German veterans, is taken by some of the more fatuous among our leaders to be an indication of his approval of National Socialism. Wishful thinking. I also believe the Führer mistaken in seeing in the Duke's tour of our country in nineteen thirty-seven any evidence of similar approval. May I remind you that a distinguished list of world leaders has visited the Reich. Does that make them all incipient Nazis?"

"So—your opinion of the Duke is that he wouldn't have the slightest interest in our overtures?"

"He has a considerable amount of German

blood in him, he speaks our language fluently, and I believe he likes us. But it is my opinion, for what it's worth, that this liking does not extend to the Nazi Party. There, have I shocked you?"

"Not at all, Herr Admiral. I asked for your opinion and you have been good enough to give it to me. I shall respect the confidence."

They started back toward the car. Canaris said, "My final word. Examine the Duke's record in the First World War. Gallant in the extreme. In spite of his father's orders that he was to be kept out of action when on the Western Front, he loved nothing better than being with the Tommies, which was why they knew him and came to love him. A basic reason for his extraordinary popularity. He always made straight for the trenches. Did you know that his aides once made an official complaint? They said it was all right for him, but the trouble was they had to follow him into the shellfire too."

"Now that I like," Schellenberg said. "That tells me more about the man than anything."

"Walter, in this matter, the Führer is hopelessly wasting his time. Here is a man who renounced a throne rather than betray the woman he loved. Do you really imagine that such a man could betray his country?"

* * *

At Estoril, in the pink stucco villa above the sea, the Duchess of Windsor sat beside the swimming pool. She was reading *Wuthering Heights,* one of her favorite novels, and was so absorbed in the action that she was not immediately aware that the Duke had emerged from the house onto the terrace and was standing beside her.

She glanced up and removed her sunglasses. "Why, David, you startled me."

"What are you reading?"

"Wuthering Heights."

"Good God, that Brontë woman again. How many times is that?"

"It's like an old friend. Extremely comforting in times of travail."

He sat down in the deck chair opposite, and she reached for the glass jug on the tray.

"Lemonade?"

"I could do with something a little stiffer, but why not?"

"Nonsense, David, you know you never drink before seven o'clock. What's happened?"

She reached across the table and took his hand. He forced a smile. "You always know, don't you, Wallis? I've had a telegram from Winston. He's finally found me a job. Governor of the Bahamas. Nicely tucked away three thousand miles from the action."

"Will you take it?"

"I'll have to. I won't have them push us into a bottom drawer. It must be the two of us together. Man and wife with the same position. They don't seem to be willing to offer us that in England. So, the Bahamas it is."

"My dear David," she said. "There's a war on, and I'm sure the question of my position doesn't loom very large on the agenda."

"But it does with me, Wallis, don't you see? I can never alter on that score." He shrugged. "It hurts a little, that's all, that they can't find anything of more importance for me to do."

He got up and walked to the terrace and stood there gazing out to sea. As she watched him, the sense of waste was so overwhelming that she had to fight to hold back the tears.

FOUR

SCHELLENBERG was back in his office within half an hour. As he was taking off his coat Frau Huber entered. She was considerably agitated.

"We've been looking for you everywhere. You didn't give any indication of where you'd gone. General Heydrich is very angry."

Schellenberg said calmly, "I thought he knew every move I made before I did. Where is he now?"

"With Reichsführer Himmler. I phoned through the moment you came in. They're waiting for you."

She was trembling a little, for she liked Schellenberg more than she dared to admit, for some strange reason admired the fact that nothing seemed to matter to him.

"Calm yourself, Ilse." He kissed her gently on the mouth. "I'll manage. Not just because I'm cleverer than they are, which I am, but because I don't take it seriously. I'll be back for coffee within the hour; you'll see."

When he was ushered into the ornate office on the first floor at Prinz Albrechtstrasse, he found Himmler seated behind a large desk, a stack of files in front of him, a surprisingly nondescript figure in a gray tweed suit. The face behind the silver pince-nez was cold and impersonal and it was difficult to imagine what went on behind those expressionless eyes. In many ways a strangely timid man who could be kind to his subordinates, loved animals, and was devoted to his children and yet a monster, responsible for almost all of the terror and repression that the Reich visited on its victims.

Heydrich was standing by the window, and he turned, his face angry. "Where on earth have you been, Walter?"

Before Schellenberg could reply, one of the several telephones rang. Himmler answered it, listening for a few moments, then said, "Insert in the appropriate file," and replaced the receiver.

He removed his pince-nez and rubbed a finger between his eyes, an habitual gesture. "So, General, your conversation in the Tiergarten with the Herr Admiral Canaris was interesting?"

"So that's where you've been?" Heydrich said. "Playing cat and mouse with that old fool again? I gave you a certain task, Walter, as you well know."

"Which I was following through."

Himmler said, "The Windsor affair, I presume? You may talk freely. General Heydrich and I are as one in this matter."

"Very well," Schellenberg said. "I made out a report of my meeting with Foreign Minister Ribbentrop as you suggested."

"Yes, I've already received it," Heydrich said impatiently.

"Then I worked my way through the Windsor file to form an opinion in the matter."

"And?"

"It was not enough," Schellenberg said. "It occurred to me that it would be a good idea to sound Admiral Canaris on the matter. I happen to know that most Thursday afternoons he goes riding, so I went to the Tiergarten and found him there."

"You had no authority to do such a thing," Heydrich exploded.

Himmler stilled him with a wave of the hand. "What was your primary reason for doing this?"

Schellenberg took his time in replying, playing it very carefully indeed. "A difficult question, Reichsführer. A matter of some delicacy."

"My dear Schellenberg, I respect your tact in this matter, but within the walls of this office there is nothing you cannot say. Not only because I am your Reichsführer, but also because we are all three men of the SS. Members of a common brotherhood."

"Come on, Walter," Heydrich said. "Speak out."

"Very well. I suspected that Reichsminister Ribbentrop had not been entirely honest with me. It seemed logical that he would have approached the Abwehr first and yet he made no mention of the fact."

"I see." Himmler's voice was very soft now and he smiled in a strangely satisfied way. "And had he?"

"I'm afraid so, Reichsführer."

"The rotten little bastard," Heydrich said.

"Leave it, Reinhard. Another nail in his coffin. But continue, Schellenberg. What did the Admiral have to say?"

Schellenberg told them, holding nothing back, for there was no need to do so. Himmler made occasional notes on a memo pad. Finally, he put down his pen.

"So—the Herr Admiral sees no good in this affair?"

"So it would seem."

"And you?"

There was a silence as they both waited for his reply, and Schellenberg knew that he was on dangerous ground now. Choosing his words with care, he said calmly, "But Herr von Ribbentrop made it clear that the whole business was to be carried through at the Führer's express command. He has even provided me with the necessary written authority. The Reichsführer must see that I cannot possibly question an order from the Führer himself. My personal opinion doesn't enter into the matter."

Heydrich turned away abruptly to conceal his smile, but Himmler was positively glowing with approval. "I could not have put it better myself. He carries the burden for all of us. The destiny of Germany rides on his shoulders."

Schellenberg said, "So, you also wish me to proceed in this matter, Reichsführer?"

"Most certainly. You will travel to Lisbon as soon as arrangements can be made, by way of Madrid, I think. A consultation with our Ambassador there, Von Stohrer, would be useful."

Heydrich turned from the window. "One

point, Reichsführer. Lisbon is alive with secret agents of every nationality, and General Schellenberg will be known to many of them. I have every faith in his ability to defend himself from the front, but I think it essential to have someone to protect his back. With your permission, I'll assign two or three of my best men."

"Not necessary," Himmler said. "I'll take care of it personally. The Gestapo, I'm sure, will be able to provide exactly the operatives we're looking for."

"As you say, Reichsführer."

"Good. You may leave us now, General Schellenberg. I'm sure you have many preparations to make. I'd like a further word with you, Reinhard, on another matter."

Schellenberg went out quickly and returned to his office. He was sweating slightly and lit a cigarette. A moment later Frau Huber came in with a cup of coffee.

"See, Ilse?" he smiled. "I told you there was nothing to worry about."

As he raised the cup to his lips his hand was trembling.

As always after such an episode he needed action and went down to the firing range in the basement which was presided over by an SS Sturmscharführer named Reitlinger. The tar-

gets against the sandbags at the far end were
of charging Russian soldiers, not Tommies, an
affectation of Himmler who still cherished the
hope of some sort of compromise with a people
who were, after all, an Aryan race.

"Action, Horst. That's what I need," Schellenberg said. "What have you got?"

"The new Erma police submachine gun, General. Just in this morning."

Schellenberg emptied it in short bursts, firing from the waist, cutting a couple of the targets in half. The noise was deafening.

As it died down, he placed the weapon on the
firing bench. "A butcher's gun. What I need is
something more subtle—a silent killer, if you
like."

Reitlinger smiled and moved to the armorer's
cupboard, for he knew very well what Schellenberg, who was a superb pistol shot, meant. He
returned with a Mauser 7.63 mm Model 1932,
with the latest adaptation, a bulbous silencer,
a weapon specially developed for German counterintelligence operatives.

"Now this is more like it."

Schellenberg hefted the weapon in his hand.
It held a ten-round magazine which he emptied
fairly rapidly, putting two shots squarely in the
middle of five of the targets. The only sound
was a series of dull thuds.

"Very neat," Heydrich said, appearing behind him, "but surely you're losing your touch, Walter? Two shots each instead of one?"

"A wounded man can always shoot back," Schellenberg said. "A second shot will almost invariably finish him off. I like to cover my bets."

"You said that as if it were a stage direction." Heydrich held out a hand. Reitlinger rammed a fresh magazine into the Mauser and passed it to him. "Yes, Walter, I am more than ever inclined to believe that is what you are—an actor. Rather a good one, by the way."

He emptied the magazine, aiming each shot carefully. "That was an outstanding performance you gave just now in the Reichsführer's office. Quite brilliant. Exactly calculated to please."

Reitlinger had moved to a position by the door which placed him out of earshot.

"And what did you expect me to say—the truth?"

"Which is?"

"That this whole thing is a waste of time. I've read that file, I've talked to Canaris, and they've completely miscalculated their man. The reports from Von Stohrer in Madrid about the Duke's sympathetic attitude. Cocktail gossip by Spanish aristocrats with fascist sympathies who want to believe he thinks as they do. That's the whole trouble. Everyone wants to believe he's on our side, and they manufacture the evidence by a kind of wishful thinking. If the Duke of Windsor said Beethoven was his favorite composer, some idiot, even in his own country, would take that to be an endorsement of the Nazi Party."

"So, you don't think he'll be interested?"

"Not in the slightest."

"Then you'll have to persuade him, won't you?"

"And what on earth is that supposed to achieve?"

Heydrich said, "When we occupy England he would have to do as he's told for the simple reason that it would be the best way he could serve the interests of his people."

He looked down toward the targets. "I haven't done very well, have I?"

"Not really." Schellenberg rammed in another clip. His arm swung up, he fired twice without apparently taking aim, and shot out the eyes of the center figure.

"And now you're angry," Heydrich said. "I wonder why?"

Schellenberg put down the gun. "We all have our off days. Do you mind if I go now? I've work to do."

"Not at all. You can pick me up at eight-thirty."

"What for?"

"This Winter girl. I'd like to see her in the flesh. The Garden Room, I think you said?"

"All right." Schellenberg walked to the door, which Reitlinger opened for him. "I'll want one of the silenced Mausers during the next couple of days. One hundred rounds in ten clips. Make up a pack for me and deliver it to the office."

"Jawohl, Brigadeführer."

Schellenberg went out, and when Reitlinger turned he found Heydrich examining the center target.

"Astonishing," he said. "Both eyes at fifty paces. Could you teach me to do that, Sturm-scharführer?"

"I'm afraid not, General," Reitlinger said. "It is not a talent which can be taught. You've either got it, or you haven't."

"Ah, well," Heydrich said. "He *is* on my side." He opened the door and smiled. "At least, I hope he is."

Lina Heydrich was away for the summer at the charming thatched-roof chalet off the Baltic coast on Fehmarn Island which Heydrich had built for her in 1935. He himself continued to live, with the help of a cook and housekeeper, at their Berlin house, which was in the exclusive Zehlendorf quarter bordering on the Grünewald forest.

Schellenberg picked him up there at eight o'clock in one of the special department Mercedes with two uniformed SS men up front on the other side of the glass partition. One to drive and the other to "ride shotgun," an expression coined by Heydrich himself, who was fond of a good Western film.

As they drove down toward the center of the city Heydrich seemed morose and out of sorts.

"Uncle Heini," he said, referring to Himmler by the disrespectful nickname by which he was known throughout the SS, "was not exactly being solicitous when he jumped in on my suggestion about providing you with bodyguards. Unless I'm very much mistaken, you'll have a couple of hand-picked Gestapo goons breathing down your neck."

"And reporting every move I make three times a day by long-distance telephone to the Reichsführer personally. Yes, I'm well aware of the possibility," Schellenberg told him.

"I don't know why, but at a time when things have never looked better, I have a feeling that they are beginning to go wrong for us—for all of us."

"And why should that be?"

Heydrich hesitated, then leaned forward to check that the glass panel which divided them from the driving compartment was firmly closed.

"This is in confidence—total confidence, Walter, but the truth is, I have my doubts about Sea Lion."

"You mean you don't think the invasion of England will take place?"

"I have a nasty feeling the moment has already passed. To be frank, the Führer's decision to halt the Panzers on the Aa Canal in Belgium, and thus allow the remnants of the British Expeditionary Force to escape from Dunkirk, was a military error of the first magnitude."

"And now?"

"Russia. I think that is the way his mind is increasingly turning. I have reason to believe he already has a contingency plan in mind."

"And you don't think it such a good idea?"

"Do you?"

Schellenberg shrugged. "Happily, I don't have to make that kind of decision. If you want my opinion, I'd say that the trouble with a Russian campaign is not particularly the Russian Army. It's the limitless distances, supply lines thousands of miles long, ferocious winter weather. Look what happened to Napoleon."

"I know," Heydrich said. "I have nightmares about that." They were traveling along the

Kurfürstendamm now and he wound down the
window and peered out. "Not what it was in the
old days—nothing is. I was at the Gloriapalast
Theater for the premier of *Blue Angel* in nine-
teen-thirty. What a sensation, and when Die-
trich appeared onstage the crowd went wild.
Believe me, Walter, those legs of hers were the
eighth wonder of the world."

"I can imagine," Schellenberg said.

"You've no idea what this town was like.
There was the Ring Club which only allowed
membership to those who'd served at least three
years in jail. The Silhouette, the Always Faith-
ful, and the Paradise which was filled with the
most glorious transvestites in gorgeous dresses,
high heels, lipstick. Not that my own tastes
ever ran in that direction."

Schellenberg said nothing, simply lit another
cigarette and let him ramble on.

Heydrich said, "One can only hope this Garden Room and your Hannah Winter can supply
us with a decent evening's entertainment. It
would make a nice change."

Hannah had already changed, ready for the
first show, and went in search of Uncle Max,
whom she had not seen since the previous evening. She found him in his office doing the
books.

She kissed him on top of the head. "Had a good day?"

"Not too bad. And you?"

"I stayed in bed most of the morning. Did some shopping this afternoon."

He took both her hands in his. "What we talked about last night, Liebchen? You'll do as I say? Leave with Connie and the boys on Monday."

"And you?"

"I'll follow as soon as I can."

"Uncle Max, you're a Jew in a city where Jews are treated as badly as at any time in the last two thousand years. I don't even understand why you came back when any Jew with sense was trying to get out."

"I'm American, Liebchen. And so are you. They don't want trouble with Uncle Sam— they've got enough on their plate, so they treat us a little differently. I don't say they like it, but that's how it is."

She shook her head. "There's more to this than meets the eye. Much more."

"Twenty minutes to show time," he said. "Make us some coffee, like a good girl."

She went out into the small kitchen off his office, leaving the door ajar. She lit the gas and filled the coffeepot with water, then lit a cigarette and sat on a high kitchen stool and waited for the water to boil.

There was a knock on the office door; it opened, then closed again violently. She heard her uncle say in German, "Irene, for God's sake! Haven't I told you never to come here?"

"I'd no choice, Max. Something happened today that was rather special."

Hannah stood up and moved so that she could see through the partially open door into the office. Irene Neumann unbuttoned her coat, raised her skirt and took the folded copy of the Windsor report from her stocking.

"I was put on temporary duty in the copying room today. I had to make copies of this for Heydrich. It's a report of a meeting between Schellenberg and Von Ribbentrop concerning a plot to kidnap the Duke of Windsor."

The kitchen door swung open and Hannah stepped into the room. Irene Neumann turned pale. "Oh, God!" she said.

"No, Irene—it's all right." Max squeezed her hand reassuringly. "This is my niece, Hannah. Completely trustworthy, I assure you. Now, let me have a look at this."

He read it quickly, then passed it to Hannah. "So—now you know. Go on—read it. This is the sort of thing that keeps me here."

Her brain seemed to be dulled with the shock

of it. She started to read the report and at the
same time was aware of Irene Neumann and
her uncle speaking in low tones.

As she finished, she heard the woman say,
"Will Moscow be interested?"

"Perhaps. On the other hand, I might be able
to pass it on through the American Embassy.
Difficult, though. The Gestapo have forty or
fifty men watching the place constantly. You'd
better go now. How did you come in?"

"By the stage door."

"Leave the same way." He kissed her on the
cheek. "Look after yourself, Irene. I'll be in
touch."

When Irene Neumann left by the stage door
it had started to rain. She paused to button her
overcoat and found an old beret in one pocket
which she pulled on.

There was a street lamp bracketed to the wall
at the end of the alley, giving the SD man, on
surveillance duty inside the delivery truck
parked on the corner, a clear view of her as she
walked toward him. He managed to take several photos of her before she turned into the
main street and disappeared into the evening
crowds.

* * *

"Uncle Max—you're a Communist?"

"Labels," he said, "are meaningless these days. The only question that matters is which side are you on. Look, try and understand. In New York, after twenty-five years, I owned a hotel and two nightclubs. Everything paid for and I had half a million dollars in the bank I didn't know what to do with. I was bored. So, I got involved with a Zionist organization that was trying to do something about what was happening to our people in Germany. Your mother knew nothing about it. I came back here in thirty-seven to help organize an escape line for Jews. I gradually got drawn into the other side of things. The only people who are really doing anything worth doing are the Socialist Underground, and by their very nature their links are with Moscow."

"And Frau Neumann?"

"Irene is a dedicated Communist. Not a card-carrying member. What they call a sleeper. Available to party orders since she was a seventeen-year-old student. She really believes Karl Marx walked on water and she loathes the Nazis. She's a clerical worker at Gestapo headquarters. There are people like her in positions of trust all over the country. You'd be surprised."

"And this?" She held up the report.

"I told you Schellenberg was important, didn't I?"

"But this business about trying to win the Duke of Windsor over to their cause. It's nonsensical. He'd never do such a thing."

"I agree, but Schellenberg's instructions seem real enough. If necessary, he's to kidnap the Duke and Duchess. It's as simple as that." He smiled. "You see, Liebchen. It's now more important than ever that you leave here Monday and make your way to Lisbon."

"Taking this with me?"

"You'd probably do better to memorize it."

Suddenly, she was filled with a fierce exhilaration. "You know, Uncle Max, being a Jew never really meant all that much to me until I came here and saw how Jews were treated. It was all right for me. Good clothes, position, an American passport. But I've had to walk by while old ladies with yellow stars on their coats have been kicked into the gutter by animals in uniform. God, but it would be nice to hit back for a change."

"You'll do it, then?"

"Why not." She folded the report, raised her skirt, and slipped it into her stocking as Irene Neumann had done. "I'll read it again later."

There was a knock at the door and Vogel, the headwaiter, looked in, holding a bunch of red roses. "I thought you'd like to know we've got distinguished company tonight."

"And who would that be?" Max Winter asked.

"Heydrich himself and General Schellenberg." Vogel handed the roses to Hannah. "These are for you, with General Schellenberg's compliments, and will you join them after the show?"

The Garden Room was not particularly busy. Vogel gave Heydrich and Schellenberg a booth that was usually reserved for guests of the management.

"Champagne," Heydrich said. "Krug. Two bottles and put more on ice."

"Certainly, General."

Vogel bustled away and Heydrich looked the place over. As usual with such clubs, there were a number of pretty young hostesses available, seated at the bar. He looked them over with the eye of the true connoisseur.

Vogel appeared with the champagne and Heydrich said, "The blonde, third from the end of the bar. Tell her to come over."

The girl came immediately. Heydrich didn't ask her name. Simply told her to sit down and poured her a glass of champagne. Then he pulled back her skirt and stroked her silken knees while he talked to Schellenberg.

Connie and his boys were playing "Some of These Days," and Heydrich drummed out the tempo on the edge of the table with the fingers of his free hand.

"Excellent—really quite excellent. You know, Walter, one of the more fatuous requirements of our present system is that it expects me to consider Negroes as my inferiors—rather unfortunate in my case as I adore Louis Armstrong, the music of Duke Ellington, and the piano playing of Fats Waller."

Schellenberg said, "The Jewish situation creates the same personal difficulties, don't you find. I mean, almost every mathematician or musician or scientist of note seems to be a Jew, and rather large numbers of them have left. I wonder just how long we can stand that?"

Heydrich frowned, which hardly surprised Schellenberg. He was well aware of his superior's dark secret, which was that his maternal grandmother, Sarah, had been Jewish.

"That kind of talk will get you into nothing but trouble, Walter. There are times when I despair of you. Times when a definitely suicidal strain shows through." He refilled Schellenberg's glass. "Here—drink up and shut up!"

The trio started to play a little louder, Uncle Max's voice boomed out, and a moment later Hannah emerged onstage and started to sing.

A great many of her numbers were in English, which was what the crowd expected. She worked her way through a number of popular songs of the day including "The Continental," "That Old Feeling," "Time On My Hands," a Noel Coward number, "Mad About the Boy," and ended with a really beautiful rendition of "These Foolish Things" that had the diners standing up and cheering.

Schellenberg had been totally absorbed and was on his feet applauding madly when he glanced to one side and noticed Heydrich still sitting down, one arm around the young girl, frowning up at him in a strangely calculating way.

As the applause died down, he said, "Careful, Walter, you're letting your enthusiasm run away with you. I think you like this one—too much, perhaps."

Schellenberg nodded to Vogel, who went and spoke to Hannah, who had stopped beside the piano to talk to Connie. She came across, pausing here and there to speak to well-wishers.

He stood up. "You were marvelous—truly."

He held her hands tightly for a moment, and she responded in spite of herself. "Thanks—I enjoyed doing it and that's usually good for the audience."

"General Heydrich, may I present Fräulein Hannah Winter?"

Heydrich didn't bother to get up. "Excellent, Fräulein. Really very, very good." His manner was cool enough to border on the offensive. He said to Schellenberg, "Actually, Walter, I've decided to have an early night. I'll take the car and send it back for you—if you want to stay on, that is."

"Yes, I think I will."

"Suit yourself." Heydrich got up, clutching the blonde girl firmly by one arm. "Fräulein— a pleasure."

Hannah and Schellenberg watched them go. He poured her a glass of champagne. "You have another show?"

"Yes, in an hour."

"May I escort you home afterwards?"

She put a hand on her thigh, aware of the folded report that she had pushed into her stocking. It gave her a strange feeling of power over him so that she smiled and said yes and was aware of that familiar hollow feeling of excitement.

"Your General Heydrich," she said. "Does he usually take bar girls home with him?"

"Frequently."

"He should beware of young Lotte. The word

I heard was that she was having to see the doctor."

Schellenberg laughed. "We have a saying in the SS. A soldier's pay—a soldier's risks."

She leaned forward, a sudden urgency in her voice. "You're not like him—like the rest of them. I don't understand."

He took her hand and said gently, "Are you familiar with a song called 'Moonlight on the Highway'?"

"Yes."

"I have a record of it sung by the English crooner Al Bowlly. It is an especial favorite of mine. Will you sing it for me?"

"If you like."

"I love good jazz singing. Billie Holiday was my favorite—until now. Your trio is really quite excellent."

"Connie and the boys. Oh, yes—terrors with the girls. Women seem to be their main spare-time interest."

She got up and he said, "I'll see you later?"

She didn't reply. Simply nodded and walked away.

Max was waiting impatiently in her dressing room. "What happened, for God's sake?"

"Nothing much. Heydrich was rude and left with young Lotte. I hope she gives him gonorrhea. Schellenberg was rather nice. Gave me champagne and asked to take me home."

"And what did you say?"

"Yes."

"You're crazy."

"Not really. I'm intrigued, that's all."

There was a knock on the door and Connie looked in. "Here we go again."

She kissed her uncle on the cheek. "You worry too much."

As she started for the door, he said, "By the way, can I have your passport? I'll get your exit visa and money in the morning."

"Top drawer of the dressing table," she said and went out.

Her second show was even more successful than the first and she ended, as Schellenberg had asked, with the hauntingly beautiful "Moonlight on the Highway."

He waited for her outside the club beside the Mercedes which had returned to pick him up. It was after two o'clock now, the streets were deserted, and the water carts were out.

When she finally emerged from the club she'd changed into sweater and slacks, over which she wore a fur coat.

She said, "It's only half a mile. Do you mind if we walk? It helps me unwind."

"Not at all."

He nodded to the driver, and as they started to walk the Mercedes crawled along behind at the edge of the curb.

"New York, Chicago, Paris, Berlin," she said. "All different by day, but at night, the same fresh smell. The same rain on the wind."

"And always the feeling that just around the corner at the end of the street something strange and exciting is waiting."

"That's it exactly," she said and took his arm.

"Twenty was a good age," he said. "One could sniff that cold bracing nip in the air on those autumnal evenings and actually believe that life was full of a kind of infinite possibility."

They continued in silence for a while and then she said, "I asked you a question earlier and you didn't answer. Will you answer me now? For some reason, it's important."

"It's simple really," he said. "First, I was a medical student, then I became a lawyer. I also spoke several languages and yet there was no work for me, you know this? No work for thousands of young Germans like me. If I could have done what I wanted, I would have gone into the theater because I suspect I am the kind of neurotic who is a natural-born actor. So—I joined the ultimate theatrical company—the SS."

"That's not good enough."

"It was a job—it was a nice uniform. It was having respect from people where there had been none before."

"From kicking old Jewish women into the gutter? From running concentration camps. I thought that the prime function of your SS."

They had reached the block in which her apartment was. He said, "Hannah, it's easy to climb on the merry-go-round. Not so easy to jump off once it starts moving. I'm afraid that's true for most of us in Germany today."

"Then I'm sorry for you."

She turned and ran up the steps to the front door. Schellenberg stood there for a while, then went to the Mercedes and leaned down.

"You can go home, boys, I'll walk."

It started to rain again and he pulled up the collar of his leather trench coat, shoved his hands into his pockets, and started to walk, his face grim.

FIVE

At TEN o'clock the following morning, Heydrich was at his desk, working his way through a mass of correspondence, dictating replies to Frau Huber, when there was a knock on the door and Schellenberg entered, carrying a couple of files. There were dark smudges under Heydrich's eyes as if he had not slept, and the paleness of his face was accentuated by the fact that he was in full black dress uniform.

"I'm due at the Führer's weekly conference at the Chancellery at eleven," he said. "And I've this lot to attend to. Can it wait?"

"Not really," Schellenberg said. "Priority One, which means a memo is already on its way to the Reichsführer."

Heydrich frowned. "Go on."

"The Winter affair. As you know, we've had a photographic surveillance team working on his club for some time. Last night they came up with a new face."

He laid a selection of photos on the desk. They showed Irene Neumann leaving the stage door of the Garden Club and walking up the alley. The one taken as she was actually passing the truck was very good indeed.

"Do we know her? Is there something on file?"

"I'm afraid so. You know Schultz in photography with that encyclopedic memory for faces? He recognized her instantly. You're not going to like it one little bit."

"Tell me the worst."

"She's a clerk in Central Records."

Heydrich looked at him in astonishment. "You mean here?"

"I'm afraid so. Here's her file."

He opened it and placed it on the desk. There were the usual double identity photos of Irene Neumann pinned to the inside cover. Ilse Huber, who had got up on Schellenberg's entrance, had been standing quietly at the side of the desk awaiting Heydrich's instructions. She could see the photos plainly.

She said, "Excuse me, Obergruppenführer, I know this woman, but she doesn't work only in

Central Records. I saw her yesterday in the copying room on temporary duty."

"Are you certain?"

"Oh, yes. I'd just done the confidential report on the meeting between General Schellenberg and Reichsminister von Ribbentrop. I went to have the usual three copies done. As I didn't recognize her, I asked her who she was."

There was a heavy silence. Schellenberg said gently, "You stayed with her, Ilse, while she made those copies?"

"Of course I did," she said. "Standard procedure with confidential documents. You know that, General." And then she remembered and her face sagged.

"Go on!" Heydrich said. "The truth."

She whispered. "The phone rang and I went to answer it. She actually brought the copies in and put them on my desk."

Heydrich slammed a clenched fist against the desk. "Out of my sight. You're finished—finished. Do you hear?"

She hurried from the room weeping. As the door closed, he said, "So, the Neumann woman could have run off an extra copy of the Windsor report."

"Almost certainly," Schellenberg said.

"So it's curtains for that damn Jew, Winter," Heydrich said viciously. "And that niece of his."

"Oh, I don't know." Schellenberg had spoken as a reflex more than anything else. "There's no necessary connection between her and her uncle's activities. Why should there be? I had her under surveillance as a matter of course, naturally, but..."

"Is that so? Well, I'm afraid I don't share your opinion." Heydrich quickly read through the file on Irene Neumann and shook his head in disbelief. "Clean as a whistle. Look at that background. Her father was a major of artillery, killed on the Somme in nineteen sixteen. Iron Cross, First Class. And her uncle, for heaven's sake. A fighter pilot with Richthofen. Awarded the Blue Max in nineteen seventeen."

"And died of tuberculosis four years after the war. She's forty years of age. A practicing Catholic. Lives alone with her mother."

"Full security clearance, as one would expect with such a background." Heydrich was bewildered. "I don't understand."

The internal phone rang and he answered it. "At once, Reichsführer." He replaced the receiver with a sigh. "He wants both of us—now. And he wants her file."

Himmler examined Irene Neumann's record in silence while Schellenberg and Heydrich stood before his desk like schoolboys awaiting their headmaster's verdict.

Heydrich said, "I just can't understand it, Reichsführer. Full security clearance, as you can see. An impeccable record."

"Which is hardly relevant," Himmler said. "That her father and uncle served their fatherland so gallantly only adds fuel to her shame." He closed the file. "And the fact that she was given full security rating shows a lack of intelligence on the part of the clearance officer concerned that I find astonishing. You will find out who it was, have him stripped of rank and transferred to a penal unit at once."

"Of course, Reichsführer," Heydrich said eagerly.

"Yes, the flaw in the woman's background is instantly clear to anyone with the slightest perception. According to the file, she went to Paris to do a postgraduate degree in French in nineteen twenty-one. Remember what a hotbed of Communism the Sorbonne was at that time? All that student agitation?"

"I see now," Heydrich said. "Of course. She could be a sleeper for our Moscow friends."

"I should have thought it obvious." Himmler turned his attention to Schellenberg. "She'll deny it, of course, but do you think she took a copy of the Windsor report?"

"I believe so, Reichsführer. Logic would indicate that."

"Explain."

"We've had a surveillance unit working on the Garden Club for some months, and she's never shown up before, which makes sense. An agent like her, so importantly placed, must be used with care. The reason for her appearance last night had to be one of supreme urgency."

Himmler said, "I agree entirely. So, Winter may now be taken into custody. And this niece of his, of course."

And again, Schellenberg spoke too impulsively. "I must point out, Reichsführer, that on the basis of my own experience, I believe the young woman to be entirely innocent in this affair. There is also the difficulty that she is an American citizen."

Himmler interrupted, "But it was my understanding that she was born in the Reich, as was Winter himself."

"Yes, but..."

"Which makes them German citizens, Schellenberg. The Führer has been most explicit on this point."

There was quiet in the room for a while and he sat there, staring down at the file. Finally he looked up. "Wait outside. I wish to speak to Obergruppenführer Heydrich alone."

Schellenberg went out. When the door had

closed behind him, Himmler said, "He has formed an attachment for this girl, am I right?"

"Reichsführer, Walter Schellenberg is the most able officer under my command."

"I did not ask you for a reference. I asked whether in your opinion he has formed an attachment for this Winter girl."

"Very well, Reichsführer. I regret to say that I think he has."

"I thought so. I have a nose for these things. Under the circumstances, he must, of course, take no further part in this affair. I would suggest that you handle it personally, Reinhard."

"With the greatest of pleasure, Reichsführer."

Heydrich hesitated. Cold and calculating by nature, his most marked characteristic a total inhumanity, he seldom cared about anybody— yet Schellenberg was different. Irritating, but true.

"Reichsführer, I trust this doesn't indicate any change in your attitude toward Schellenberg. His loyalty is unquestioned, believe me, and he has been of great service to the Reich."

"Undoubtedly." Himmler leaned back. "General Schellenberg has all the qualities. A brilliant intellect, gallant soldier, cultured, witty. Humane by nature. In the field of counterespionage, one of the most able minds in Europe. He is also a romantic fool."

"But his record, Reichsführer, is impeccable. A good party member."

"Which means nothing. Anyone can pay that kind of lip service. Frankly, I doubt his devotion to National Socialism considerably." He raised a hand. "Don't worry, Reinhard. He's too good a man to discard—yet," he added. "Now let's have him back in."

A moment later, Schellenberg was once again in front of the desk. "I've decided you will start for Spain tomorrow," Himmler said. "Under the circumstances, you will hand all relevant information concerning the Winter affair to Obergruppenführer Heydrich."

"As you say, Reichsführer."

"Good. You may go."

Back in his office, Schellenberg stood at the window, smoking a cigarette, trying to control his anger. But the truth was, however unpalatable it might be, that he could not do anything for Hannah Winter now.

He turned and noticed a box on his desk. When he opened it he found it contained the Mauser he had asked the armorer for, plus the additional ammunition. There was also a requisition slip for him to sign. As he slipped a round into the magazine, the door opened and Heydrich came in.

He paused on seeing the Mauser. "I suppose you'd like to use that on me?"

"She's clean," Schellenberg said. "I'm certain of it."

"Then she's got nothing to worry about. Good God, man, I've done you a favor, don't you see that? I knew we were in trouble when I heard you actually left her at the door of her apartment last night. Walks through the streets in the rain in the early morning. Like something out of one of those absurd films UFA are always churning out. What were you trying to do—commit suicide?"

Schellenberg put the Mauser back in the box. "All right. What now?"

"You'll fly to Spain tomorrow by special courier plane. Paris, San Sebastian, Madrid. All fixed up. Your Gestapo bully boys will be provided later today."

"Thanks very much."

"And now I must interrogate Irene Neumann. Only don't interfere, Walter, promise me that?" He sounded almost plaintive. "It really would be something of an improvement if you started doing as you were told for a change."

Irene Neumann sat on a chair in front of Heydrich's desk, her hands folded firmly in her lap, her face expressionless. Two SS men guarded the door.

She was not afraid. The shock effect of her sudden arrest had had a numbing effect so that she was not really capable of taking anything in. This was a moment she had always known might come—and yet, now that it was here...

Heydrich entered. He sat down behind the desk, opened her file, and sat there reading it, totally ignoring her.

"So—Fräulein Irene Neumann?"

"Yes, Obergruppenführer."

"You know why you are here?"

"I have no idea. If there has been some mistake in my work..."

He pushed the surveillance photos across the desk. "You, coming out of the Garden Room last night."

For a moment only, her iron reserve failed and what she felt showed on her face.

"Yes, you might well look dismayed. This is the day your chickens come home to roost. The day you've dreaded the thought of all these years." He got up and stood at the window, looking out, his back to her. "The copy of the Windsor report which you stole. You showed it to Winter, of course. That was the object of your rather injudicious visit, but was his niece with him at the time?"

"I have nothing to say."

"It doesn't matter. They'll be joining you shortly, both of them."

She made no reply.

He came around the desk and took her chin gently in one hand tilting her face. "You will tell me, Fräulein, in the end. I promise you."

Hannah went shopping during the morning and had her hair done. When she returned to the apartment, the porter had a telephone message for her asking her to meet Uncle Max at the club, which surprised her, for during the day it was locked up tight. There was seldom anyone there before six o'clock in the evening.

She found the stage door open. As she went in his voice called, "Is that you, Hannah?" and he looked out of his office. "Close the door and lock it, will you?"

She did as she was told, then followed him into the office. "What did you want to see me about?"

"Arrangements for your trip. What have you done with the report?"

She patted the top of her thigh. "Still in my stocking. I didn't like to leave it at the apartment. I spent a couple of hours memorizing it during the night. Do you want me to destroy it?"

"I don't know," he said. "It's the sensible

thing to do, but on the other hand such a story might not be taken seriously without the evidence. Let me think about it some more."

"Have you got my passport?"

"Of course." He took a large envelope from his inside breast pocket and produced a passport. "There. You'd better check it."

"But this is French," she said. "There must be some mistake."

"Take a look."

She opened it. The usual photo stared out at her, the personal details were as always, except in two important respects. Her name was given as Rose Lenoir, born in Paris. She was still described as a singer.

"I don't understand."

"I had it made up for you. If you have any trouble trying to cross into Spain or Portugal as Hannah Winter, you switch identities. Your French is good enough if you keep it short, the conversations, I mean. I have a friend who specializes in such things. It's a real work of art. Dozens of immigration stamps, see? German, Belgian, French, Spanish, Portuguese. Some nice and clear, some carefully smudged so you can't make out the date properly. It's okay. Your real passport is in here as well, plus contingency money in francs and pesos. Enough to get by on and a letter of credit for two thousand dollars on American Express at Lisbon."

He put the false passport back into the envelope.

"You seem to have thought of everything," she said.

There was a knock at the stage door. Uncle Max slipped the envelope back in his breast pocket, opened the desk drawer, and took out a Walther automatic pistol. He moved to the window and peered out. A young man wearing a tweed cap and blue overalls stood there whistling cheerfully. He was carrying a bulging leather Gladstone bag of the type used by tradesmen.

Max slipped the Walther into his pocket and went out into the passage. "Who is it?" he called.

"Herr Vogel?"

Uncle Max opened the door, leaving the security chain in place. "He isn't here. What is it?"

"Mansteins—plumbers. Something wrong with the hot water supply in the number two kitchen, wherever that is. I wouldn't know. Haven't been before. Herr Vogel rang this morning."

Max undid the chain and let him in. "First door on your left is the main kitchen. Straight on through and you'll find the number two."

"All right, leave it to me." The young man

had very bright blue eyes. He winked impudently at Hannah and disappeared into the kitchen.

Max followed her back into the office. There was the sudden roar of an engine outside in the alley, the squeal of brakes, pounding feet.

"Oh, dear God," he said and grabbed her by the shoulders. "If anything happens, if we get separated, I'll be at a firm of monumental masons called Hoffer Brothers in Rehdenstrasse. It's close to the zoo. Now follow me and do everything I say."

As they went into the passage the young man with the bright blue eyes emerged from the kitchen. He was holding an Erma police submachine gun.

"All right, Dad, against the wall, nice and slowly. Nothing foolish."

Pounding started on the door, he glanced briefly toward it, and Uncle Max flung himself at him. The young man reversed the Erma and struck him under the ribs and Max went down with a cry of pain.

The young man stood over him, back turned to Hannah. "You know, I'd kick your head in for that if you weren't so valuable."

There was a heavy porcelain lamp on top of the filing cabinet by the door. Hannah picked it up in both hands and brought it down with all her strength. It smashed across his head and he went down on his knees.

The battering on the door had risen to a crescendo. As her uncle looked up at her, face still twisted in pain, she said desperately, "Uncle Max, what are we going to do?"

He was breathing with some difficulty. "The wine cellar. Help me to the wine cellar, and bring that thing with you."

He nodded to the Erma and she picked it up gingerly and helped him to his feet. They reached the end of the corridor, and he started to unbolt the grill leading to the wine cellar steps. Behind them, the stage door fell from its hinges, and the entrance suddenly seemed jammed with SS.

Hannah turned and swung up the Erma instinctively, her finger tightening on the trigger. She had never fired any kind of weapon in her life before, and the Erma was like a living thing in her hands, ripping plaster from the passageway walls, driving the men in the doorway into the alley.

She kept on firing convulsively, the Erma bucking so violently that she fell back against Uncle Max as he got the grill open. He lost his balance and slid down the wooden stairs to the cellar below.

Hannah had dropped the Erma. She was on

her knees now and screamed, "Uncle Max—are you all right?"

She saw him get to his feet. "Quickly!" he called.

A hand grabbed her right ankle as she tried to get up. She half turned and found the young man with those bright blue eyes crawling toward her, his blond hair sticky with blood.

"Oh, no you don't, you bitch." He punched her in the stomach. Behind him, other SS men poured into the passage and ran to help him.

As for Max, there was nothing he could do except turn and stagger into the next cellar, thankful to be able to walk. He closed the stout oaken door and rammed home two steel bolts, then moved on between rows of wine bottles.

Behind him, a furious pounding sounded on the door, but they were too late, for he had anticipated this situation for some time and had made every preparation.

Against the end wall of the third cellar, there was a wooden cupboard. Inside were a hat, a raincoat, a large flashlight, and a briefcase containing various false documents and a supply of money in several currencies.

He put on the coat and hat, then pushed the cupboard to one side, disclosing a neat hole in the brickwork. He picked up the flashlight and the briefcase and clambered through, turned, and pulled the cupboard back into place.

He was in the cellars of a disused warehouse at the rear of the club, which had been standing empty, ready for demolition for three years now.

A couple of minutes later he was unbolting a door revealing a flight of steps leading up into a small yard, crammed with the rubbish of years.

He opened the gate and peered out. The alley outside was completely deserted. He closed the gate behind him and walked rapidly away.

At that same moment in Estoril, the Duke and Duchess of Windsor were entertaining Miguel Primo de Rivera, the Marqués de Estella, who had driven over from Madrid especially to see them.

As the servants cleared the remains of luncheon from the table beside the pool, De Rivera took out his watch.

"Time passes so quickly in good company, but I'm afraid I must leave soon. I must start back for Madrid today. I've an important official engagement tomorrow."

"What a shame," the Duchess said.

De Rivera smiled and said to the Duke, "I wonder whether Your Royal Highness could spare me a few moments' conversation before I go? In private."

The Duke looked faintly surprised, but smiled as courteously as always. "Yes—why not. We shan't be long, Wallis."

It was, in fact, half an hour before they returned and then only for De Rivera to take his leave. He kissed her hand, promising to come again soon, and departed. The Duke lit a cigarette and moved to the edge of the terrace, leaning on the marble balustrade, frowning as he looked out to sea, an expression of intense preoccupation on his face.

"And what was that all about?" she demanded.

"I'm not sure. It was really most extraordinary. He'd heard of my Bahamas appointment from official sources in Madrid. Had even discussed it with Franco."

"But why, David?"

"Do you know, Wallis, he urged me not to go. Said I could still have a decisive role to play in English affairs. He actually said we'd be better off going to stay in Spain. Would be made officially welcome."

"Would you rather do that?"

"Too complicated. You see, present indications are that the Spaniards don't intend to enter the war on the side of the Nazis, but they might well use England's present plight as an excuse to demand the return of Gibraltar. I certainly don't want to become a pawn in that kind of game."

"So you don't trust De Rivera?"

"I trust the Madrid Falangists no more than I would any Fascists. There could be more to this than meets the eye, Wallis. Much more."

His eyes crinkled in that inimitable smile and he put an arm about her waist. "There's a certain excitement to it all, though, I must admit that."

SIX

THE CELL was quite small, the concrete walls whitewashed. Almost antiseptic in its cleanliness. There was a light recessed into the ceiling, a small iron cot with no mattress. A cold, white concrete womb.

Hannah sat on the edge of the cot, her mind still so numbed by events that she was unable to take any of this in. There was a dreamlike quality to everything. It was like one of those nightmares half-remembered in the morning and fast fading. That desperate scramble in the passageway at the club, the machinegun bucking in her hands, the smell of cordite. And Uncle Max? Where was he now?

Her stomach still hurt from the blow, and

when she touched it bile rose in her throat so that she had to get up and move to the bucket quickly.

Heydrich, watching through the spyhole, nodded to the SS guard and the Gestapo interrogation expert he usually used on such occasions, Major Berg.

"All right," he said to Berg. "Open up."

The sound of the bolts being withdrawn was of no significance to Hannah. She still sat there, staring at the wall, so that Berg had to drag her to her feet.

Heydrich lit a cigarette and stood facing her, legs apart. He was wearing dress uniform, a devil in black, but his voice when he spoke was dispassionate.

"You're quite a girl, aren't you? Two of my best men dead. Three more in the hospital—one on the critical list. They trained you well, your people. The fluent German. Just like a true Berliner, very convincing."

"I was born in Berlin. So were my mother and grandfather. You know this. We always spoke German at home in New York when I was a child."

He turned to Berg. "Strip her. Thorough search. I'll be back in a few minutes."

He went out into the corridor and along to the main guardroom, where he telephoned through to the Charité hospital to find out how the survivors of the debacle at the Garden Room were doing.

When he returned to the cell, Hannah was standing in the center of the room, quite naked, her hands folded in front of her. Her clothes were laid out neatly on the bed.

The purpose of such an exercise, the use of male interrogators, was part of a psychologically devised procedure designed to induce feelings of guilt and shame in the victim and to increase the alienation syndrome. Hannah, however, showed no emotion and simply stared at the wall.

"We've struck gold, Obergruppenführer," Berg told him. "I found this in the top of one of her stockings."

Heydrich unfolded the copy of the Windsor report. "Excellent. Now we're really getting somewhere." He tapped her gently on the face with the folded report. "Didn't know what I was talking about, eh? I've just been in touch with the hospital and you know what they told me? A third man, the one of the critical list, has just died." He grabbed her hair savagely and swung her head from side to side. "Bitch—that's murder three times over."

But she felt no pain—no pain at all. It was

as if this were happening to someone else—as if she were standing outside looking in.

"Your uncle—where did he go?"

Her voice seemed to come from a great distance away like a faint echo. "I don't know."

Heydrich pushed her away. "Get your clothes on," he said harshly.

Berg said in a low voice, "She's still in shock. I've seen it often enough before with people like her. They live with the thought of it for years—being caught, I mean. When it comes, they try to reject the fact. Pretend it isn't happening. It's a kind of withdrawal."

"Then we'll have to shake her out of it, won't we? You go and see how they're getting on with the Neumann woman. I'll be along in a moment."

Berg went out and Heydrich stood there watching as she dressed slowly and methodically, still with that strange vacant look on her face. She really did have an excellent body, he told himself. As she sat down to pull on her stockings, he felt the excitement rise in him.

Himmler was in uniform for once when Schellenberg went into his office. The Reichsführer glanced up. "So—I did you a service by removing you from further active participation in the Winter affair."

"So it would appear, Reichsführer."

"In normal circumstances, you would almost certainly have been in charge of the special action group which went to the Garden Room. Whoever was will be severely disciplined. A deplorable business."

"I must agree."

"Three dead. Two wounded. A surprising young woman. You were obviously wrong about her."

Schellenberg gave him the reply he was seeking. "I'm afraid so, Reichsführer."

Himmler said, "A little humiliation is good for the soul on occasion, but I didn't bring you here to discuss that. I have selected the two Gestapo men I wish to accompany you to Lisbon as your bodyguards."

He spoke briefly on the internal telephone. A moment later the door opened and two men entered. They were large and powerfully built and wore rather nondescript gray suits of conventional cut. One was bald and the other wore glasses. Schellenberg recognized the type instantly, for all the Reich security services were full of them. Ex-police officers, more used to moving among criminals than anything else.

"Sturmbannführer Kleiber," Himmler said and the one in the glasses clicked his heels.

"And Sturmscharführer Sindermann. General Schellenberg, you know."

"A pleasure, Brigadeführer." Kleiber didn't bother to put out his hand.

"I have already explained the purpose of your visit to Lisbon to Major Kleiber," Himmler said. "In fact, I have specially selected him for this task, as he does speak Portuguese. He was stationed at our Embassy in Lisbon with the security staff for three years before the war. His local knowledge will be most useful to your purposes."

"I'm sure it will be," Schellenberg said.

"And now I suggest you show Major Kleiber the Führer's order under which you are acting so that he knows exactly where he stands."

Schellenberg produced it from his wallet and passed it to Kleiber. The major read it, face expressionless, showed it to Sindermann, then handed it back.

"So you see, gentlemen. Any order you receive from General Schellenberg is an order from the Führer himself."

"Understood, Reichsführer."

"Excellent." Himmler smiled up at Schellenberg. "No need for you to stay. I'm sure you have your desk to clear before leaving. Arrangements to make."

Schellenberg withdrew, aware that it was

simply a polite way of getting rid of him so that
Himmler could give Kleiber his special orders.
Not that it mattered, for he could well imagine
what they must be.

"Are you a religious man, Kleiber?"

"Not really, Reichsführer."

"General Schellenberg is. He had a strict
Catholic upbringing. People like that tend to a
rather moralistic attitude which can cloud their
judgment on occasion. They see people as being
more important than causes—that sort of thing."

"I see, Reichsführer."

"I wonder if you do? In this Winter affair, as
I have explained to you, the General seems
more concerned with the young woman involved than with the damage her uncle's activities have caused to the Reich. To be blunt,
Kleiber, General Schellenberg is a most excellent officer. In the field of counterespionage
there is probably no one in Europe to excel him.
However, it seems to me that on occasion he
lacks a certain conviction, and I'm not entirely
happy about his attitude to the Windsor business."

"I see, Reichsführer."

"There are times, Kleiber, when one must be
prepared to go for the throat if necessary. I'm
relying on you to see that Schellenberg does. As

your Reichsführer I have a right to demand
your unquestioning loyalty in this."

"You have it, Reichsführer, I swear it," Kleiber said.

There was a knock at the door, and Heydrich
entered, a smile of triumph on his face. He put
the copy of the Windsor report on the desk in
front of Himmler.

"Hidden in her stocking."

Himmler examined the document. "So, Schellenberg *was* wrong about her?" He looked up at
Kleiber. "You see what I mean?"

Heydrich opened the door of the cell and
moved in. She was sitting on the edge of the
bed again, fully clothed.

He said, "All right. On your feet. Follow me."

She hesitated, and he lost patience, grabbing
her by the arm, and pulling her out through the
door. He pushed her along the white-painted
corridor. It was quiet enough and seemed to
stretch into infinity, and then she became
aware of a dull rhythmic slapping, strangely
remote as if it came from a long way away.
Heydrich paused outside a cell door and slid
back a metal gate. He pushed Hannah's face
against it so that she had to look inside. Irene
Neumann, her dress ripped to the waist, was
sprawled across a bench while a couple of heav-

ily muscled SS men beat her systematically across back and buttocks with rubber truncheons. The woman arched in agony. Berg stood watching.

Hannah came back to life then, the horror of it like a blow in the face. "You see?" Heydrich said. "All she has to do is tell us the truth about the Windsor affair. Answer a few questions about your uncle. It would appear she prefers to die."

He pushed Hannah's face against the metal gate again, and she struggled to free herself. "No, let her go! Make them stop."

"All right, you answer my questions for her."

"No—I don't know anything."

"We'll see, shall we?" He opened the door and said to Berg, "Hold it." He turned to Hannah. "Now—each time you fail to answer, we start again. So you see, you will be the instrument of her pain."

She was terrified now, and it showed clearly in her face.

He said, "You and your uncle—have you been working together ever since you arrived from America?"

"No," she said.

"Then how do you explain the copy of the Windsor report?"

"It was an accident. I overheard Fräulein

Neumann talking to him." Her mind roamed desperately, seeking the right way to frame her answers. What to give and what to hold back.

"You weren't aware before then that your uncle was working against the Reich?"

There was no need to inject fear into her voice, it was already there. "I swear it."

"And the Windsor report? Why was it secreted on your person?"

"He'd already arranged for me to return home to America via Lisbon. He thought I could take the report and show it to the Duke of Windsor."

"You've read it? You are familiar with its contents?"

Her mind, sharpened now by every instinct of self-preservation, told her that to reply honestly to this question might make him believe her lies also.

"Yes—I memorized it."

"On his instructions?"

"Yes."

"Where is he now?"

"I don't know."

He snapped his fingers, and the truncheons started to descend again. She clutched at his arm. "It's the truth, I swear it. He ran away—left me. We didn't even have time to talk."

And he believed her, staring down into her contorted face, aware, with a fierce anticipatory joy, of the power he held over her. He nodded to Berg. The beating stopped.

"And the Negroes—the musicians. Were they in any way involved?"

"No."

"Good." He turned to Berg. "Put her back in her cell. Then take the other to number three. Any medical treatment she needs. Hot bath, food. You know what to do."

One entire anteroom was crowded with the staff of the Garden Room, who were being interrogated individually. Connie Jones, Billy Joe, and Harry Gray were sitting together in a corner, talking in low tones. They had already gone through the interrogation process and weren't too happy about it.

"I asked to see someone from the American Embassy," Connie said, "but it didn't do any good. This whole thing stinks. All those questions about Hannah and Max."

"The way I see it," Harry Gray said, "we'll be lucky to make it out of here in one piece."

Heydrich entered and walked through into the office, ignoring everyone. The young SS officer behind the desk jumped to his feet.

"Anything?" Heydrich demanded.

"All clean, Obergruppenführer."

"And the Negroes."

"Sturmbannführer Kleiber interrogated them
and was satisfied they know nothing. They are
due to leave for Madrid via Paris in the morning. I have their tickets here along with their
passports."

"Very well," Heydrich said. "Keep them in
custody overnight, then put them on the train.
Official deportation."

"And the reasons, Obergruppenführer?"

"Associating with enemies of the state," Heydrich said, and he turned and went out.

He found Schellenberg in his office, signing
letters.

"So, Walter, you're ready to leave?"

"Just about," Schellenberg told him. "The
Reichsführer introduced me to my chaperons,
by the way. A pretty pair. The excuse for one
of them, Kleiber, is that he knows Lisbon, which
is nonsense. The Reichsführer knows perfectly
well that I've been to Lisbon on three occasions
during the past two years. I have all the contacts that I need."

Heydrich placed the heavily creased Windsor
report on the desk in front of him. "Tucked into
the top of her stocking. You were wrong. She
was going to take it to Lisbon to the Duke for
her uncle."

"Not by design," Schellenberg said. "I knew

she was going to Lisbon. The travel agents reported the ticket booking as they always do in
the case of foreign nationals. That was before
the report was stolen. Before my interview with
Ribbentrop."

"You mean you think she could just be an
innocent tool? Yes, that is a possibility. She
assured me that the Negro musicians who work
with her know nothing about the affair."

"And you believed her?"

"They were in a room by themselves that was
wired for sound for a good hour. Their conversation indicated honest bewilderment, and
Kleiber interrogated them and seems satisfied.
I've ordered their official deportation. It saves
trouble with the Americans. After all, they are
black, and there is a certain, rather tiresome
liberal section of the American press that might
kick up a fuss if we keep them in custody."

"And the Winters?"

"Only naturalized Americans, Walter. German born—Jewish to boot. You should see the
photos of the dead and wounded in the alley
outside that club. Goebbels will have a field day
if we ever need to publish. Nobody wants that
kind of trouble. I think you'll find that the
Americans wouldn't want to know, not with the
present international situation. We are, after
all, the ones in the saddle."

"Yes, I suppose you're right," Schellenberg said.

"I invariably am. The girl will have to be interrogated further, but I'll handle that myself."

Schellenberg knew what that meant. Realized that Heydrich was taking a perverted pleasure in telling him, for his sexual habits were well known.

"Actually, Walter, I'll do her a favor. You bring her up for me. Talk to her like a Dutch uncle. Make her see sense. She might listen to you. It could save her a lot of grief."

"As you say, Obergruppenführer. The Green Room?"

"But of course," Heydrich said, smiling.

When the door of the cell was unlocked and Schellenberg entered, Hannah looked up at him without speaking.

"Have you nothing to say?" he said.

"Not to you—ever again. I made a mistake. I thought you were different, but I was a fool. What do you want, anyway?"

"Heydrich told me to bring you to him."

She stood up wearily. "Does that mean what I think it does?"

"Usually."

She followed him into the corridor. He glanced

at his watch. "Ten minutes to seven. Just getting dark."

"How interesting."

"Oh, but it is. SS organization is meticulous. Everything on time." They had mounted the cellar steps and emerged into the foyer where two guards stood at the main door. "At precisely seven o'clock each night, the Chancellery messenger goes out through that door with dispatches for the Führer and others."

They were climbing the staircase to the first floor now.

"Yes," Schellenberg said. "The situation reminds me of an astonishing story I heard from Paris recently. It seemed a young woman was arrested, suspected of being a member of some French Resistance group. They took her to Gestapo Headquarters at Rue des Saussaies at the back of the Ministry of the Interior. Someone left her alone in an office for a moment. Apparently, she picked up a file and walked out. Waited near the foyer till some general or other went out of the front entrance, then followed a minute later, telling the guard she had a file the general had forgotten. Once outside, she was up the nearest alley in a flash. Not too good for the guard, of course, but that's life."

She stared at him, eyes wide. "What kind of man are you? I don't understand?"

He opened a door at the head of the stairs adjacent to Heydrich's office and ushered her in. It was plainly furnished and painted green with a desk, some filing cabinets, and a divan against one wall. There was a clock over the far door.

"See the time," Schellenberg whispered. "A minute to seven. Two minutes after would be about right." He managed a smile. "I hope you can count."

He crossed to the far door, knocked, and opened it. Heydrich was sitting behind his desk. He stood up and came across at once.

"Ah, Walter, you've brought Fräulein Winter, I see. Thank you very much. You can go now. Better get on with your packing."

"Obergruppenführer."

The door closed softly behind Schellenberg. Heydrich stood watching her, a slight smile on his face. He took out a cigarette case, selecting one. He had all the time in the world. He might as well savor it. Behind and above him the second hand of the clock reached seven and moved on.

Heydrich said, "Come here." She hesitated, panic moving inside her. "I said, come here!"

She started forward, but as she got close the phone rang sharply in his office. He swore softly, turned, hurried through, and picked up the receiver.

"Hello? What is it?"

There was a heavy silence and then a muffled voice said, "Record Department?"

"No, it damn well isn't."

He slammed down the receiver and went back into the other room. It was quite empty, the door to the outside corridor standing slightly ajar.

It just wasn't possible. Such a thing could not have happened—not to him. He wrenched open the door and went down the staircase to the foyer on the run.

"Have you seen a girl?" he demanded of the guards. "Pretty—dark-haired. Tweed skirt and a white blouse."

"That's right, Obergruppenführer, she went out just a minute ago."

"Without a pass? How could she?"

The guard who had been doing the talking looked scared now. "She had a file in one hand, Obergruppenführer. Asked if the Chancellery messenger had left yet? I told her he'd just gone through, and she said to catch him as there was an important dispatch for the Führer."

Heydrich ran down the steps into Prinz Albrechtstrasse, but it was quite dark now. Of Hannah Winter, there was no sign.

He had no choice, of course. He had to put
out a red alert, and then he went in search of
Schellenberg, whom he found in his office dictating a last few letters to Frau Huber.

"Out!" Heydrich snarled at her. "Outside—
now!"

She went, pale and frightened. Schellenberg
said, "What is it?"

"She's gone, Walter. That little Jewish bitch.
I went into my office to answer the phone—a
minute only—when I went back, she'd cleared
off."

"But how could she get past the front door?"

"Apparently she went out just after the Chancellery messenger passed through. Told the sentry she had another urgent dispatch for him."

Schellenberg said, "Breathtaking in its im-
pudence, you must admit that."

Heydrich glared at him. "Walter, if I thought
for a moment that you had anything to do with
this."

"I left her in your care, Obergruppenführer,"
Schellenberg said gravely. "Since then, I have
been dictating letters to Frau Huber, as she will
testify."

Which was not entirely true, for when he had
asked her for a cup of coffee it had taken her
at least two minutes to go for the thermos she

always kept in her office, ample time for him to phone Heydrich's office on the internal line.

"All right. All right," Heydrich said. "But what am I going to say to the old man?"

There was a timid knock on the door, and Frau Huber peered in. "Well?" he demanded. "And what do you want?"

"Sorry, General, but the Reichsführer is on the telephone. He wants to see you both—now."

Once outside, Hannah had walked quickly away, but not too quickly, expecting at any moment a voice to call her back. She turned into the first street on her right, only then starting to hurry.

It was early enough for there to be plenty of people about and a warm enough July evening for a girl in a short-sleeved blouse and skirt not to look out of place.

She had no money for a cab, of course, and had to keep walking, working her way toward the zoo, which took about forty-five minutes. Once there, she asked directions to Rehdenstrasse from the woman who kept the coffee stall outside the zoo gates, who was fat and friendly enough to give her a cup of coffee on the house while she scrawled directions on the back of a dirty menu card with a pencil stub.

Rehdenstrasse was a rather mean street of

old decaying warehouses beside the River Spree.
Halfway along, a sign lit by a single bulb said
Hoffer Brothers—Monumental Masons. The large
wooden gates that gave access to the yard were
locked, but not the small side gate.

She stepped inside and recoiled in horror as
a row of ghostly figures loomed out of the shadows. And then she laughed, a release from nervous tension as she realized what they were.
Religious images, angels and cherubim of stone,
standing amid a cluster of crosses.

She moved on toward a warehouse on the
other side of the yard. Light showed faintly behind a curtain at an upstairs window. There
was a narrow door, which opened to her touch,
and she found herself facing a flight of wooden
stairs.

Quite early in the war, German counterintelligence had developed a sophisticated range
of radio-bearing detection apparatus and mo-
bile direction-finding units, able to search the
major cities of Western Europe to find and eliminate the secret transmitters operated by various underground organizations.

There had been only one such transmitter left
in action in Berlin for some time now and that
only because, under Max Winter's orders, trans-
missions to Moscow had been at irregular in-

tervals. The location of the equipment had always been moved immediately after each period of use.

The present situation was at Hoffer Brothers, which was what the firm was called although there was only one brother still alive: Otto, who had lost a leg at Verdun and had been a member of the Communist Party since 1920.

Max had gone straight there on leaving the club. Had sent for the radio which had been delivered by van together with the operator, a young man named Haupt, a new recruit who suffered from tuberculosis and had therefore avoided army service.

And then a dreadful error had occurred: Haupt, in a moment of mental aberration, had mistakenly switched the set, which worked on alternating current, onto direct current, rendering it unusable. He was out now trying to obtain replacement parts. In fact, when Max heard the door open, he thought it was Haupt returning, and then he went to the head of the stairs and saw Hannah.

She sat drinking the coffee Otto Hoffer provided, aware of her uncle's voice on the phone in the next room, muted through the wooden wall.

"A miracle," Otto Hoffer said. "To walk out

of Gestapo Headquarters just like that. That's really left those bastards with egg on their faces. God, but I wish we could splash it across the front page of the *Berliner Zeitung,* just so people would know."

The door opened, and Uncle Max entered. "It's all fixed. You leave for Paris in one hour by road. From there, you'll be taken on to Spain by special courier. From Madrid, you can take a train to Lisbon—no trouble."

"But how?" she said. "You make it seem so simple."

"There's an underground route I've used to get important Jews out of Berlin many times before. The people I use aren't idealists. They're crooks who do the whole thing strictly for cash. I like that. It means you know exactly where you are."

"I see."

He took a man's trench coat from behind the door. "Wear this. A little big, but you can belt it up tightly." He took the envelope she had last seen in his office from his inside pocket. "Train tickets—no use now, of course. Both passports, francs, pesos, and the letter of credit for Lisbon."

"You've thought of everything."

"Not quite." He took a pistol from a drawer, a Walther PPK. "This thing is loaded with seven rounds. If you want to fire it just yank back the slider at the top like this. After that, you just keep pulling the trigger. I'll put the safety catch on. Flick that off, and it's ready for action."

"Do I really need it?"

"You might. I'll give it to you later. Now let's get moving."

They walked through a series of back streets, crossing the River Spree on an iron bridge at one point, and finally turned into a street very similar to Rehdenstrasse. Mainly warehouses and office blocks.

A faded sign said, *Eagle Wine Company. Import-Export*. Max knocked at the gate. It was opened instantly and a small, bald-headed man in a brown overall coat looked out.

"Hello, Scherber," Max said and moved through, followed by Hannah.

"Five minutes," Scherber said. "That's all you've got, then I want you off the premises."

"Understood." Max passed him a wad of hundred-mark notes held together by an elastic band. "Are the boys ready?"

"Over here."

Hannah saw that they were in a large, dimly lit warehouse. A tanker stood at the far end by huge double doors, and two men stood beside it, smoking cigarettes.

"The Dubois brothers," Max said quietly. "Paul is the older one with the bad teeth. Henri is the one who does as he is told."

Henri was young, no more than twenty-one, and wore a tweed cap and leather jacket. "So this is our cargo?" he said in bad German. "Delightful."

His brother said sourly, "What about our cash, Max? Two thousand francs, that's what we agreed."

Max counted it out. "The boys transport wine in bulk."

"And anything else going," Henri said.

"I used to deal with them extensively before the war. Then there was a gap for obvious reasons. But they're back in business now."

"All those Krauts in Paris like German wine," Henri said. "And we aim to please."

"Cut out the funny stuff and show her where she goes," Paul Dubois told him. "And let's get out of here."

Henri opened the cab door, pulled back the double seat, and lifted out the liner. There was a trap door behind, and he reached inside and switched on a light.

"All the comforts of home: mattress, coffee in a thermos, ham sandwiches. I hope you're not too Jewish to eat them, but it's all we've got and I didn't know you were coming until an hour ago. Sorry about the boxes. A few special items for the Paris black market."

"I'll be fine," she said.

"Twenty hours," Paul Dubois said. "We take it in turns to drive."

Hannah turned to Max, who took out the Walther and handed it to her. "You'll need this now."

Henri said, "Don't you trust us?"

"Not really," Max said. "She's killed before. She can again if she has to." He kissed Hannah on the forehead. "When you get to Lisbon, go straight to the man himself."

"I won't let you down."

"I know you won't, Liebchen. Go with love. Stay well."

She was crying now, as if aware by instinct that she would never see him again. She clambered through the hatch into the narrow space inside the tank. She had one final glimpse of him standing there, and then Henri shut the trap. She sat down on the mattress and looked around her as the engine roared into life and the tanker lurched forward.

SEVEN

IT WAS ten o'clock when Irene Neumann finished the meal that had been served to her in the comfortable room they had taken her to after her bath. The gray-haired woman who had looked after her had been quite solicitous.

"I think they must have made a mistake, dear. It happens," she said.

Certainly the meal had been excellent, and Irene, wrapped warmly in a toweling robe, had enjoyed it in spite of the fact that she ached from her beating and could barely sit down.

Fried chicken, potatoes, real coffee, and a cognac to finish off. She started to come to life again, and then the door was kicked open with a crash and Berg and two SS men rushed in and grabbed her. They threw her into the corridor, and Berg pulled her head back by the hair so that she could look up at Heydrich.

"Oh, no, Irene," he said. "Not you. You've done your share. It's the turn of the person in the next cell now."

They dragged her along the corridor to the next door, and he opened the metal gate so that she could lock inside. An old, gray-haired, frail-looking woman sat on the bed.

"Frau Gerda Neumann, your mother, I believe—age seventy-one," Heydrich said. "Is it true she has a bad heart?"

Ten minutes later, Irene was sitting in front of the desk in his office, telling him everything she knew.

It was just after midnight when Haupt returned to the Hoffer Brothers' warehouse with the necessary spare parts. Max Winter had been back for a good three hours.

"My God, it took you long enough."

"I was lucky to get what I wanted at all," Haupt told him.

Max yawned, went to the window, and peered out through the curtain. He stiffened suddenly, aware of a movement down there among the monuments.

"Otto," he called to Hoffer, "I think we have company."

"I'll check the front," Hoffer said.

He opened a cupboard, took out a Schmeisser machine pistol, and went down the rear stairs to the main warehouse. He didn't bother to switch on the light, but cocked the gun and walked toward the doors in the darkness, and then the night was filled with the roaring of an engine and the doors smashed inward as a heavy troop carrier burst through.

The offside front wheel caught Hoffer a glancing blow, bouncing him against the wall. His fingers squeezed the trigger of the Schmeisser convulsively, and at least half a dozen weapons fired at him in reply, tearing him apart.

Max, at the top of the stairs, knew that it was over. He stood there waiting for them, the Walther ready in his hand. He started to pray aloud, that most common of Hebrew prayers recited three or four times a day by any Orthodox Jew; the last prayer he utters on his deathbed:

Hear, O Israel; the Lord our God,
the Lord is one.

The first stormtrooper who appeared he shot through the head, then someone shoved a

Schmeisser around the corner and fired a long
burst, hitting him several times so that he fell
down the stairs.

The rest of the attack group trampled over
his body and went up the stairs on the run,
followed by Major Berg. A moment later they
reappeared, dragging Haupt.

Heydrich was standing at the bottom of the
stairs looking down at Max Winter. He glanced
up as Berg descended.

"He's dead, which is a pity. What have you
got there?"

"Radio operator. An incompetent, by the way,
who switched a set that works on alternating
current onto direct. He was in the middle of
trying to repair it."

"So, you've transmitted messages today?"
Heydrich demanded.

Haupt was terrified and showed it. "No—not
a thing."

Heydrich turned to Berg. "No sign of the
girl?"

"None, Obergruppenführer."

Heydrich said to Haupt, "Has there been a
young woman here this evening?"

Haupt looked bewildered. "A woman? No—
no one like that."

"All right, Berg. Take him back to Prinz Albrechtstrasse, and see what you can get out of

him. I'll take the men with me and see what we turn up at the other address the Neumann woman gave us."

But the Eagle Wine Company was in darkness, and there was no sign of Herr Scherber, the proprietor, at his small apartment near the Charlottenburg Station where he lived alone. His next-door neighbor indicated that he frequently stayed out all night.

The interrogators at Prinz Albrechtstrasse worked on the unfortunate Haupt for most of the night. He told them nothing because he knew nothing.

It was seven o'clock in the morning when Scherber was finally located in a steam bath off Kurfürstendamm, a place much frequented by homosexuals. Once caught, he sang his heart out.

There was quite a crowd in Himmler's office for nine o'clock in the morning: Heydrich, Schellenberg, Major Kleiber, and Sindermann.

Himmler said, "So, we know Winter didn't have time to pass on any information about the Windsor affair by radio, and the missing copy of the report is in our hands."

"Which means that the only other source of information on the subject is that damned girl."

"At present on her way to Paris in the company of two French black marketeers," Himmler said.

"We have the address where they are to deliver her at the other end," Heydrich said. "A café called the Golden Coin in Montmartre. I'll arrange for the Paris office to provide a reception committee. They'll be delighted. Quite a coup. This should uncover an entire underground courier service for them."

"No, tell them to wait," Himmler said. "I have a better idea." He turned to Schellenberg. "You leave for Spain this morning, flying by way of Paris."

"I was under the impression that you didn't want me to have anything further to do with this Winter affair, Reichsführer."

"True, but Major Kleiber here could take charge most adequately." He looked up at Heydrich. "Arrange it with the Paris office. When does your plane leave, Schellenberg?"

"Eleven o'clock from Tempelhof."

"I wish you luck then in the venture that lies ahead. Naturally I shall expect daily reports."

"Of course, Reichsführer."

"Kleiber, you will please stay."

Schellenberg and Heydrich went out. In the

anteroom, Heydrich paused to light a cigarette. "God, what a night. Still, it all seems to be working out in the end. You see, Walter, all you have to do is live right."

Himmler said to Kleiber, "In the matter of the Winter girl's escape last night. The fact that she was able to ask the sentry if the Reich Chancellery messenger had gone through shows an intimate knowledge of procedure here that can only indicate that she had inside help."

"General Schellenberg, Reichsführer?"

"Watch him closely, Kleiber, and report to me daily. You can phone from our Lisbon Embassy. Here is the necessary authority." He passed Kleiber an envelope.

"I understand, Reichsführer."

"Let's hope you do," Himmler said. "You may go now."

Kleiber went out, and Himmler picked up the old-fashioned pen with the steel nib that he always favored and started to note the details of the conversation meticulously in his diary.

At that moment, the wine tanker was turning off the road outside Alf on the road to Trier. Henri was at the wheel; his brother, asleep beside him, came awake instantly.

"Why are you stopping?"

"Come off it, Paul. The young lady needs a

turn in the bushes like the rest of us, and if she doesn't, I do."

Hannah had slept surprisingly soundly considering the circumstances, but she was awake now, aware of the truck slowing down and bumping over rough ground.

The trap was opened, and Henri grinned through at her. "Time to stretch your legs—or whatever else you want to do."

She was instinctively wary, ready for anything as she scrambled through. When she jumped to the ground, she slipped a hand into her pocket and gripped the butt of the Walther. "Where are we?"

"On the road to Trier. Luxembourg after that." There was a rustling in the bushes, and Paul Dubois appeared, fastening his trousers. Henri waved a hand, "The other side of the wood is yours. Quarter of an hour, then we move on."

He climbed back into the cab, and Hannah turned and walked away through the trees, going some considerable distance before she stopped.

Afterward, she moved back in a half-circle, attracted by the sound of running water, and came out among pine trees on a small promontory above a river. It was pleasant standing there, the early morning sun playing on the rushing water. There was a movement behind, and she turned to find Henri approaching.

"Ready to go?" she said.

"Time for a cigarette."

He offered her one, and she accepted it, her right hand clasping the Walther firmly, pushing the safety catch off with her thumb. He was standing very close now.

"That's the Moselle River behind you. Pretty, isn't it?"

"If you like that sort of thing," she said in French. "Personally, I'm a big city girl."

His eyes widened. "Heh, you've got a Parisian accent. How come?"

"I sang at a club in Montmartre for six months in thirty-eight. Club le Jazz. Do you know it?"

"I used to go there all the time." He ran a hand up her right arm and pushed his body against her, his voice thickening. "Hey, listen, chérie. How about you and me..."

She slipped the Walther out with an ease which surprised herself, but then she was not the girl she had been forty-eight hours before, not by any stretch of the imagination. For a moment, she could smell again the cordite in the passageway of the Garden Club as she rammed the barrel of the Walther into his stomach.

He grinned, "Now don't be silly. You know

you wouldn't," and kissed her.

She fired into the ground between his legs and he jumped back with a cry of fear.

"Careful," she said calmly. "You almost lost something."

Paul Dubois arrived on the run, crashing through the bushes. "What is it? What's happened, for God's sake?"

"Nothing," Hannah slipped the Walther back into her pocket. "A slight misunderstanding between Henri and me, but I think we know where we are now."

Paul Dubois slapped his brother across the face.

"Will you never learn? Anything in a skirt and you're like a dog in heat." He turned to Hannah. "It won't happen again, I guarantee. Now let's get out of here, and fast, just in case some inquisitive farmer heard that shot."

The Ju-52 transport was the aerial workhorse of the German army during the Second World War and it was used extensively for troop, freight, or passenger transport. Its three engines gave it a distinctive appearance, and the corrugated metal skin earned it the affectionate nickname of Iron Annie.

Schellenberg had traveled this way many times before, but in pleasanter company. Kleiber had positioned himself halfway along the plane with Sindermann at the rear by the steward's compartment, as if to emphasize the difference in rank.

Which at least left Schellenberg alone at the front, but it was hot and rather stuffy, and he was glad, after a while, to accept an invitation from the pilot to visit the flight deck.

Afterward, he went back to his seat for coffee and sat there, thinking about Hannah Winter and the trap which would be waiting for her at the Golden Coin in Montmartre. There was nothing he could do this time—he was already in too deep. There was always the possibility that she would reveal his part in her escape for, under the kind of pressure applied in the Prinz Albrechtstrasse cellars, most individuals broke in time—or died first.

He felt curiously indifferent. It was all one in the end, and he leaned forward and peered out of the window as Paris loomed below.

Kleiber appeared beside him, looking excited. "Le Bourget, General. The Führer flew in here at four in the morning of June the twenty-third with Keitel and a handful of his staff. When most Parisians were still in bed, our Führer toured their city. What a moment for Germany!"

"Marvelous," Schellenberg said. "I hope it kept fine for him."

A Gestapo major named Ehrlich was waiting for them when they went through into the VIP lounge.

"A distinct pleasure, Brigadeführer," he said to Schellenberg. "A car is waiting."

"You've had your instructions from Prinz Albrechtstrasse?"

"Yes."

"Then you'll know that Sturmbannführer Kleiber is in charge of this affair."

Kleiber said, "Naturally I would welcome your presence as an observer, General, if you can spare the time."

There was a challenge there which Schellenberg could hardly refuse. "Why not? As long as I have time to visit SD headquarters at Avenue Foch before we leave, I am entirely at your service, my dear Kleiber."

As they went out, he fingered the butt of the silenced Mauser in his pocket. If there was a melee at the Golden Coin, a stray bullet might well pass unnoticed, giving Sturmbannführer Willi Kleiber the opportunity of dying gallantly in the service of the Reich. It was a happy thought. As he got into the Citroen limousine provided, Schellenberg was smiling.

* * *

The tanker turned into the parking area beside a small truckers' café in Clichy, north of Montmartre, and Henri braked to a halt.

"Are you going to phone, or shall I?"

"No, leave it to me," his brother said and jumped to the ground.

Henri leaned back and tapped on the bulkhead. "Okay in there?"

There was a muffled reply, and he grinned and lit a cigarette.

Inside the café, Dubois went into the telephone booth and dialed the number of the Golden Coin. The receiver at the other end was picked up instantly.

"Yes, this is the Golden Coin. What can I do for you?"

It was Madame Bonnet, but there was something in her voice, he was sure of it; an instinct produced by a lifetime of bad habits told him as much.

"Would it be possible to book a table for seven tonight?" he asked. "Chicken paprika and a good Muscadet, if you could manage it."

"No, I'm sorry, monsieur. I'm afraid we shall not be open for business tonight."

Paul Dubois said calmly, "Many thanks, madame. Another time."

* * *

At the Golden Coin, half a dozen customers sat at the tables trying to look as if they were enjoying their drinks. Walter Schellenberg leaned on the end of the bar and three Gestapo agents waited behind the curtain leading to the kitchen.

Angélique Bonnet was seated at her usual place behind the desk at the side of the bar, a small gray-haired woman in a severe black dress who ruled the establishment with a rod of iron.

Her husband, called to the Reserves, had been killed at Arras. Her one consolation in life was that her son, a navigator in the French Air Force, had escaped to England.

She put down the telephone receiver and Kleiber, who had been monitoring her conversation, replaced the earpiece on its hook.

"Good."

"But of course," she said. "Soon I will have no customers left, and still I do not know what all this is about."

"A tanker filled with good German wine to be delivered here by two brothers named Dubois together with an even more interesting consignment, eh?"

It was not for nothing that Angélique Bonnet

had spent fifteen years of her youth with a provincial repertory company, and her bewilderment looked extremely convincing.

"But I know no one of that name, monsieur, and as for German wine—well, with the greatest respect, there's just no call for it here."

Kleiber looked uncertain and glanced toward Schellenberg, who said, "Have you considered the possibility that they don't actually have any connection with the establishment, but with one of the customers?"

"Yes, that had occurred to me, naturally."

"And the local police. They have been issued with details of the tanker?"

"A full description," Kleiber said stiffly. "Including the number."

"Then there should be no cause for concern." Schellenberg turned to Angélique Bonnet. "My dear madame," he said in fluent French, "I'm afraid I must trouble you once again for another glass of that special cognac. It really is quite excellent."

Paul Dubois leaned into the truck. "Right, get her out, quick," he said to Henri. "Something's up at the café."

His brother removed the panel and pulled Hannah through. She looked about her, bewildered. "Where are we? Paris?"

"Yes," Paul Dubois told her. "A truckers' café in Clichy. I think we're in trouble. Whenever we have a passenger like you to deliver, we always phone in, just before arrival. A prearranged code. I order a special meal for a certain number of people. If things are okay, she accepts the booking, the woman who runs the place."

"And she didn't just now?"

"Said she was closed tonight, and I've never known the Golden Coin to close before, not even during the first days of the German Occupation."

"So what do we do?" Henri demanded.

Paul Dubois frowned, then made his decision. "If things have gone wrong at the Berlin end, this thing could be hot," he said, slamming his hand against the tanker. "We'll leave it here and go the rest of the way on foot. If I'm wrong, if things are okay, we can come back for it later."

There was a small church on the hill above the square in which the Golden Coin stood. From its cemetery, they could see the café clearly, the striped awning above the tables on the sidewalk.

"There's a black sedan parked in the alley over there," Henri said.

His brother nodded. "Another in that build-

ers' yard to the right. Oh-oh!" he added as Major
Ehrlich, wearing a dark overcoat and trilby hat,
walked out of the café and started across the
square.

"Know him?" Henri demanded.

"I certainly do. Name of Ehrlich. One of those
Gestapo bastards from Rue des Saussaies. That
does it." He turned to Hannah. "Sorry, kid. I
don't know what went wrong, but they're waiting for us down there. You're on your own."

He nodded to Henri. They hurried away. She
was alone, standing there in the cemetery,
caught for a moment by the suddenness of it all.
But that would never do and she, too, turned
and walked away.

She knew Paris well, thanks to that six-
months' cabaret engagement before the war,
which was one good thing. She hurried through
the streets of Montmartre, down past the Gare
St. Lazare, never stopping until she at last
reached the Place de la Concorde by the Seine.

She found a coffee stall with tables arranged
around it. No coffee, only beer as it turned out,
but she bought a glass and sat down to take
stock of her situation.

She knew the city and she spoke French tol-
erably well and she did have a supply of francs,
thanks to Uncle Max's forethought, plus the

two passports, the Spanish pesos, and the letter of credit on American Express in Lisbon. And there was something else—something she'd totally forgotten until now.

With fingers that trembled slightly, she took out the railway tickets from the envelope. Berlin to Paris on the first, but the second was the important one. The berth on the sleeping car on the night train to Madrid, leaving Austerlitz Station at six o'clock.

She glanced at her watch. It was five-fifteen and Austerlitz was a good three miles away on foot. She jumped to her feet and, as she turned, saw a small delivery truck swerve into the curb. The driver, a middle-aged man in blue overalls with a drooping white mustache stained brown in the center from nicotine, tossed a bundle of newspapers onto the pavement by the coffee bar and started to move away again. Hannah ran like hell and scrambled into the passenger seat beside him.

"Hey, what's this?" he demanded.

"Please, monsieur, help me." She pulled out her passport and held it up. "See—I'm an American citizen, on my way home. I've got a seat on the Madrid Express leaving Austerlitz at six. I decided to do a little sightseeing and got lost and I'll never make it on time now, unless you'll drive me there." She pulled a wad of francs from the envelope. "I'll make it worth your while."

"Keep your money." He grinned. "American, eh? Which part? My son lives in Los Angeles. You catch your breath and sit back. I'll have you there within fifteen minutes."

When the phone rang again, Angélique Bonnet answered it as before. "For you," she said to Kleiber, as he reached for the earpiece. "Police headquarters."

The expression on Kleiber's face was like a shot in the arm to Schellenberg. The Sturmbannführer replaced the phone. "They've found the tanker," he whispered. "Apparently abandoned in the car park of a truckers' café about a mile from here."

"So?" said Schellenberg calmly. "A wasted afternoon? My commiserations, Sturmbannführer, but if I'm to have any time at all at SD headquarters, I must leave now. I'll see you back at Le Bourget at eight o'clock."

He went out and Kleiber stood there, one hand gripping the edge of the bar.

Angélique Bonnet said, "Is it all right if I start taking bookings for tonight now?"

Her face was quite calm, no sign of triumph there at all, and he turned from her and stalked out, crossing the square to where Sindermann and Ehrlich waited by the Citroen in the builders' yard.

"No good," he told them. "The French police have found the tanker abandoned about a mile away. No sign of these Dubois brothers or the girl."

"They could be anywhere by now," Sindermann said. "God knows what her next move will be."

It was Ehrlich who suggested the obvious. "We know her intention is to reach Spain, is it not so? There is a night train to Madrid leaving Gare d'Austerlitz at six o'clock."

"Ridiculous," Sindermann said. "She'd never dare."

But Kleiber's face was ablaze with excitement. "She had a booking on that train made in Berlin by her uncle. A sleeping-car berth. So did those niggers."

Ehrlich glanced at his watch. "Thirty-five minutes, Sturmbannführer, that's all we've got. I think we'd better get moving."

It was just after five-thirty when the old newspaper delivery man dropped Hannah at Austerlitz Station. It was very busy—a mixture of civilians and German soldiers—and police seemed to be everywhere.

She found the correct platform for the Madrid Express and approached the gate. There was a typed list posted on the notice board beside the ticket collector, of passengers in the three sleeping cars. Her name was there in the first-class section along with Connie and the boys, a four-berth private compartment.

But to get on the train was one thing. To be known to be on it would be foolishness of the worst kind, and if she presented her ticket, the collector would mark her off on his list.

She moved some little distance away to consider the matter. At that moment, two porters passed her, pulling a chain of rubber-wheeled trucks piled high with mail. They pushed open a wide gate giving access to the platform, and Hannah, without hesitation, followed them through, staying on the left-hand side so that she was hidden from the ticket collector.

There were plenty of people on the platform, boarding the train. She walked toward the engine and finally came to the sleeping cars. A steward was standing on the platform beside the open door that gave access to the first-class coach. He was consulting a sheet he held in one hand while a distinguished-looking man in dark overcoat and Homburg hat, with a neatly trimmed gray beard, stood anxiously beside him.

"I regret to have to say it, Count, but at the

moment, it would appear that every berth is taken."

Hannah moved on past them and ducked in through the door at the other end of the coach. And there it was, only a step away: Compartment A.

She tried the handle, but the door was locked. With a sinking heart, she tried knocking. There was a muffled voice inside, then the door opened.

"What is it?" Connie Jones started to say in French, and then his face seemed to split wide open.

"Hannah-baby."

And then she was inside, the door closing, his arms around her, Billy Joe and Harry laughing in astonished joy, and for some reason she started to cry.

The three Gestapo men reached Austerlitz at precisely five minutes to six. Harry Gray was at the small platform kiosk by the gate buying cigarettes. He recognized Kleiber at once, turned, and hurried along the platform.

"We got trouble," he said as he went into the compartment and closed the door behind him. "That guy who interrogated us at Prinz Albrechtstrasse—Kleiber. He's just turned up at the gate. He was checking the list with the ticket collector when I left."

"But I didn't come through officially," Hannah said. "I may have an official booking, but I'm not supposed to be here."

"That doesn't mean a thing. Any second now they're going to come knocking on that door. The question is, where do we put you."

There were the four berths, two on either side, and a small toilet.

Connie shook his head. "Man, you couldn't hide a cat in here."

Billy Joe turned to Harry with a grin. "Remember that time on the Chicago-Hollywood run? That big, fat white you-all from Alabama who didn't mind sharing with black folk as long as they was clean?"

"And we drove him out with disgust." Harry was grinning all over his face as he started to unbutton his shirt.

Billy Joe was doing the same. "You know the story, Connie. We told you often enough. Now get her into bed real smart."

Hannah looked bewildered. Connie said, "Do as you're told, kid, and whatever happens, keep real still."

Billy Joe and Harry were stripping off their pants as Connie pulled back the blanket and shoved her down into the bottom bunk. He pushed her against the wall, pulled the blanket over her and put a pillow on her head.

The two boys were stark naked now. Harry lay back on the bunk against Hannah and Billy Joe sprawled across him. A second later, the handle of the door jerked, followed by a thunderous knocking.

"Come on, open up! Police!"

Connie opened the door on the chain and peered out at the sleeping-car attendant. "Hey, man, what's the beef? You've had our tickets. We'd like a little privacy."

"There is a fourth reservation here in the name of Hannah Winter."

"It wasn't taken up, man—last I heard she was in Berlin."

"But you've no objection to us making sure." Kleiber appeared behind the ticket collector.

"Oh, no," Connie groaned. "Not you again. I thought we'd had all that."

"Open the door or we'll break it in," Kleiber said.

Connie slipped the chain. Kleiber pushed open the door, shoved him back across the compartment, and crowded in, followed by Sindermann and Ehrlich. The first thing he saw were two pairs of black legs intertwined on the right-hand lower bunk, Harry Gray's hands digging into Billy Joe's buttocks.

Harry said, "Whoops, we got company."

Billy Joe turned, exposing his nakedness completely. "I thought the reason we paid first class was because privacy was guaranteed."

Kleiber stood glaring at them, his face very pale. He kicked open the toilet door, gave one quick glance into the empty interior, then went out into the corridor. The others followed him, and Connie slammed the door behind them.

"May the train leave now, Sturmbannführer?" the steward asked.

"No," Kleiber said. "Not until we have checked every passenger."

They worked their way back toward the far end, inspecting each compartment, but finally had to admit defeat. As the whistle blew, Kleiber, standing by the gate, saw Connie lean out of one of the corridor windows.

"Any time, Major."

He waved cheerfully and ducked back inside. The sleeping-car attendant was coming along the corridor and Connie took out his wallet and produced two one-hundred-franc notes.

"Let's make sure that berth stays empty for the rest of the trip, okay? My friends and I—well, we enjoy our privacy."

The attendant accepted the notes with alacrity. "Certainly, monsieur, and if there is any

other way I can be of service. These Boche." He
shrugged. "They are not men of the world, eh?"

When Connie went into the compartment,
Harry and Billy Joe, with towels around their
waists, were sitting on one bunk, Hannah opposite. All three were laughing helplessly.

"That guy's face," Harry said. "I wish I had
a picture."

"Okay, children. Joke over." Connie sat down
beside Hannah and took her hand. "I got some
bad news for you, kid. It's about your Uncle
Max."

The Ju-52 climbed to fifteen thousand feet
and set course for San Sebastian, where they
were to refuel. Kleiber sat opposite Schellenberg, the disgust on his face plain as he spoke.

"What decadence. The Führer is right. The
inferiority of such races—the Negro and the
Jew—is plain."

"Interesting really," Schellenberg said, light-
ing a cigarette.

"I don't understand what you mean."

"That they should be like that, the two boys.
Possible, of course, but the impression Fräulein
Winter gave me was that they were spectacu-
larly successful with the ladies."

Kleiber glared at him, his face paler than

ever as a dreadful suspicion began to form in his mind.

Schellenberg smiled. "If you'll excuse me, I think I'll join the pilot," and he went out onto the flight deck.

EIGHT

THE TRAIN had to stop at the border town of Hendaye for the carriages to be jacked up and the bogeys changed to suit the narrower Spanish railway lines.

There was a customs check on the Spanish side of the border at Irun. Hannah stayed in the toilet while the customs officer came around with the sleeping-car attendant to check passports.

There was a short delay before they moved off again. She came out and lay down on one of the lower bunks, her eyes red, swollen from her weeping. Billy Joe and Harry simply sat there looking troubled. After a while, Connie came in with sandwiches and coffee from the dining car and sat down beside her.

"Have something to eat. Do you good."

"I couldn't."

"You've got to pull yourself together," he said.

"You just don't understand."

"Is that so? Well, let me tell you something, little white sister. This nigger served with the Harlem Brigade on the Western Front in nineteen-eighteen. We were longer in the trenches than any other unit in the American Expeditionary Force. I lost my only brother, two cousins, and damn near every friend I had in the world, and you know what it taught me? That life goes on. Now your Uncle Max—those bastards killed him. Right?"

She nodded, hands clenched.

"You gonna let them get away with that? He gave you a job to do, girl. Are you gonna do it or are you just gonna sit on your ass and cry all day?"

She flung her arms around him. "Oh, Connie, what would I do without you?"

"That's my girl. Now hear me. I've spoken to the attendant, and it appears we arrive at Madrid at nine o'clock in the morning. There's a train leaves for Portugal at nine thirty-five from the same platform. In fact, it don't leave till we get in so you can't miss it even if we're late. You can get your ticket on board. Fifteen hours to Lisbon. You get in at six-thirty in the evening."

"That's fine," she said. "Couldn't be better."

"There's the border," Harry Gray pointed out. "Could be trouble there."

"I don't see why," Hannah said. "In any case, I'll use the false passport Uncle Max gave me, just in case."

"When you get to Lisbon, if you need any help, go to Joe Jackson's American Bar. Any cab driver in Lisbon knows where it is."

"Joe Jackson?"

"We're due to play there next week. He's an old friend and a really great guy. You name it and Joe's done it. Fought against Franco in Spain with the Lincoln-Washington Brigade, and he flew fighters against the Condor Legion. There's nothing happens in Lisbon that Joe doesn't know about."

"You make him sound like some kind of racketeer."

"Let's say he's a shrewd operator and leave it at that. Now get some sleep, kid. You're going to need it."

She slept then, turning her face to the wall, trying to blot out every thought of Uncle Max. When she finally awakened to Connie's hand on her shoulder, they were in Madrid.

The Junkers had trouble in the port engine, and there was a delay of some five hours at San

Sebastian, so that it was almost ten o'clock as they swung in over the old city of Madrid and landed.

There was a car waiting to take them to the Embassy. As they drove down into the city, Kleiber said, "When shall we be continuing our journey, General? Today or tomorrow?"

"Oh, sometime this afternoon, I think," Schellenberg said. "It depends how long my business takes with the Ambassador."

"With your permission, I'd like to check the railway station."

"That train was due in an hour ago, Kleiber." Schellenberg shook his head. "You're obsessed with the idea of that girl roaming across Europe when she's most probably holed up in some attic in Berlin."

"Or she could be here in Madrid at this Club Flamenco where the blacks are to appear."

The car turned into the courtyard of the Embassy and braked to a halt. "Very well," Schellenberg said. "You can take the car. Be back here to pick me up no later than two o'clock."

At Chamartin Station, Kleiber soon discovered that the Paris-Madrid Express had arrived on time, and a few moments' conversation with the stationmaster elicited the fact that a train had left the same platform for Lisbon at nine thirty-five. The stationmaster also telephoned the taxi rank to see if anyone had picked up three Negro passengers and came up with the interesting information that Connie and the boys had been delivered to a well-known night club called the Flamenco.

Half an hour later and Kleiber was closeted with Madrid's chief of police who, in line with his country's political stance at that time, was only too pleased to assist the Gestapo.

"I believe there could be a woman named Hannah Winter on the Lisbon Express, traveling on a false American passport. A German citizen, wanted for murder. Once she is in custody, we shall apply for extradition naturally."

"The train crosses the border at Valencia al Cantara, but I can do better than that." The chief of police glanced at the clock on the wall. "It stops at Talavera one hour from now. I will have the local police board and search for this woman. In the meantime, if you would care to wait, perhaps we can enjoy a glass of wine together, and you can tell me how it is in Berlin these days."

The train had been stopped at Talavera for some time before Hannah looked out of the window and saw the police. She didn't panic, simply settled herself back in the corner and returned to her magazine. She was wearing dark sunglasses and a headscarf tied around her hair peasant-fashion. Connie had bought them for her at the station kiosk at Madrid.

There were only two other passengers in the compartment: a priest and a young woman with a baby. They all waited. Finally the door was pulled back.

Hannah kept on reading the magazine, aware out of the corner of her eye of the uniform legs.

"Señorita. Passport."

She looked up at the young police officer as if startled, then produced her French passport and handed it over.

"Rose Lenoir. You are traveling to Lisbon, mademoiselle?" he asked in halting French.

"Yes," she said.

"May I ask the purpose of your visit?"

"Business. I'm a singer. I'm to appear in a cabaret in Lisbon next week."

She crossed one leg over the other, allowing the hem of her skirt to slide well above the knee. The young policeman swallowed hard and handed back her passport.

"*Bon chance,* mademoiselle," he said and went out.

The priest looked quite shocked, the young woman amused. Hannah smiled at her, replaced her sunglasses, and returned to her magazine.

* * *

The Club Flamenco was in a small square in the old quarter of the city. When Kleiber, Sindermann, and the Embassy driver went in, the place was deserted except for an old man swabbing the floor with a mop.

"We're closed," he said in Spanish. "Open at eight o'clock tonight."

"What about the new act, the Negroes?" the driver asked.

"They were here. Went off to find a hotel. Said they'd be back at two o'clock to rehearse."

The driver relayed this information to Kleiber, who nodded in satisfaction. "All right—we'll wait."

"If you don't mind, Sturmbannführer," the driver said, "I'll phone in to the Embassy, just so they know where I am."

He went out, and Kleiber went behind the bar and helped himself to a drink while Sindermann took up station by the door.

At the Embassy, Schellenberg found himself in impressive company. There was Von Stohrer, the Ambassador, and the Spanish Minister of the Interior, Ramón Serrano Suñer, brother-in-law of General Franco. As his knowledge of German was limited, they spoke together in English, a language they all shared in common.

"Let's take our coffee on the terrace, gentlemen," Von Stohrer said. "Much pleasanter out there."

They sat around a small white-painted iron table while one of the servants served coffee. Von Stohrer waved him away. "So, now we can get down to business."

He was not just a career diplomat, but a conventional Nazi with unquestioning allegiance to the Führer. His close personal contacts with the Spanish government at every level were of tremendous importance, especially at that time when negotiations between Spain and Germany about the further conduct of the war were at a most delicate stage.

"So—what is the present problem?" Schellenberg asked.

"Perhaps, Minister, you would care to say something?" Von Stohrer said.

Serrano Suñer nodded. "Very well. So far, we have used as an emissary to the Duke, the Marqués de Estella, Primo de Rivera, who has been a friend of the Duke for a long time. I think I should stress at this stage, that the Marqués is," here he hesitated, "how shall I describe it? A man of finest honor?"

"I take your point," Schellenberg said dryly.

"To continue. The Marqués has no idea of our mutual interest. He believes himself purely to be acting for the Spanish government in the matter and takes his instructions from me on behalf of our government."

"Are you implying that he only has the welfare of the Duke at heart?"

"Exactly. They are old friends. The Duke has had to surrender his passport to the British Embassy in Lisbon. It is by now common knowledge that he doesn't relish his appointment as Governor of the Bahamas. A posting deliberately designed to get him as far away as possible. It would be understandable if he felt insulted at its lack of importance. It is more than probable that he is also under close surveillance by British Intelligence."

"So, what has De Rivera suggested to him?"

"That he move to Spain where the Spanish government would gladly grant him asylum, there to await events."

"And does De Rivera think the British would sit idly by while the Duke and Duchess pack their bags and move out?"

"No. He went to Lisbon again yesterday, to visit the Duke at Estoril. His intention is to arrange a day in the country at some convenient spot near the border. A hunting party with old friends. An obvious opportunity for the Duke and Duchess to step across before the British, or anyone else, knows what is happening."

"And if they choose not to?"

"But that, my dear Schellenberg, is where you come in," Von Stohrer said.

Schellenberg nodded. "I see. Abduction. And De Rivera is aware of this possibility?"

"No," Serrano Suñer admitted. "As I've indicated, the Marqués is acting purely out of concern for what he believes to be the best interests of an old friend. I should also point out that there is a rumor, current in Spanish society circles at the moment, that it is the plan of the British Secret Service, once the Duke is in the Bahamas, to do away with him as soon as may be. Naturally, the Marqués will convey this information to the Duke."

Schellenberg laughed out loud. "And do you seriously expect him to believe it?"

"I have it from Reichsminister von Ribbentrop himself," Von Stohrer said stiffly. "A report from a Swiss informant who has had for many years the closest of contacts with the British Secret Service."

"The Marqués will return tomorrow with details of the hunting trip, the date and so on," Serrano Suñer said. "These will be communicated at once to Huene at our Portuguese Legation who will, in turn, pass them on to you."

A manservant appeared through the French

windows and bowed. "Berlin on the telephone, Excellency."

"Excuse me, gentlemen. I'll be back in a minute."

Von Stohrer went out and Serrano Suñer offered Schellenberg a cigarette. "You looked skeptical, General, about this report from the Swiss agent concerning the British Secret Service and their designs on the Duke."

"One of the problems of intelligence work is to sift the truth from the lies," Schellenberg said. "Or what is even more difficult, to learn to recognize the distortions so that you can at least extract what little truth there is available."

"You think the Swiss may be lying?"

"There are men like him in every capital in Europe. I can see him now, sitting in the corner of some café in Geneva with a bottle at his elbow, wondering what story to satisfy his masters with this week."

The Spanish Foreign Minister said, "General Schellenberg, I know your reputation, which in your line of work is legendary, so I will be frank with you. We are anxious, here in Madrid, to see a successful conclusion to this Windsor affair for one reason only—to accommodate the German government."

"And why would this be important at this

time?" Schellenberg said. He could guess why, but preferred having the cards on the table.

"The Führer would like nothing better than for Spain to enter the war on the side of Germany. He feels very much that we owe him this if only because our triumph against the forces of Communism in the Civil War was largely due to the massive military aid we received from the Reich."

"But there is more to it than that?"

"Yes. At the moment Britain is still supreme in one respect—her navy. Our entry into the war would give Germany Gibraltar and strike the most crushing blow against the British Navy possible by denying entry to the Mediterranean."

"In return, what would General Franco require?"

"Arms, petrol, manufactured goods that are in short supply here because of the devastation of the Civil War. Also the French colonies in North Africa, particularly Morocco and Western Algeria. You understand the situation now?"

"Perfectly." Schellenberg told him. "General Franco is willing to enter the war on our side, but only after Operation Sea Lion has been concluded with the successful occupation of England. His need is to keep present discussions as drawn out as possible until that happy event is concluded. In the meantime, the abduction of the Duke of Windsor, in accord with the Führer's wishes, serves to show that the General's heart is in the right place, thus keeping everyone happy."

Serrano Suñer smiled broadly. "I couldn't have put it better myself. I see that we understand each other and, to be honest, I think that abduction will be necessary. I do not believe His Royal Highness would come willingly."

"Have you any special reason for believing that?"

"Yes, I think so. When the Duke and Duchess were here in Madrid recently, they had dinner at the Ritz with Doña Sol, the sister of the Duke of Alba. On their arrival she gave them the fascist salute. It caused something of a stir because the Duke made it quite clear that he didn't like it one little bit."

"I see."

"On another occasion, he dined with the Infante Alfonso, his cousin by marriage, who had fought in the Civil War and made a great deal of German military might. In fact, made it clear that he thought Britain finished."

"And what was the Duke's reaction?"

"He became quite incensed. Asked the Infante if he'd never heard of the English Channel." Serrano Suñer shrugged. "You may not think these

things of great importance, but to me they indicate an attitude of mind in the Duke that is
anything but favorable to your cause."

Von Stohrer returned. "That was Reichsminister von Ribbentrop himself on the telephone
from Berlin, gentlemen. I reported your safe arrival, Schellenberg. He trusts that you will carry
on to Lisbon with all speed."

Schellenberg glanced at his watch and saw
that it was almost two o'clock. "Yes, indeed. I
really must get moving. The pilot was told to be
ready to take off at two."

"I'll see you out," Von Stohrer said.

"No need. You still have much to discuss, I'm
sure. I'll be in touch at the earliest possible moment, naturally."

It hadn't gone too badly, he told himself as he
went out. He certainly knew more than when he
went in. The Great Game, some English intelligence chief during the nineteenth century had
once called it, and what a game. Walking the
razor's edge of danger. How many years of his
life had he lived like that?

And to come so close to throwing it all away
for the sake of a girl he hardly knew. Who most
certainly despised everything he stood for. That
black humor that was so often his saving grace
brought a cynical smile to his lips.

"Ah, Walter," he said softly. "Three Hail Marys and two Our Fathers for the sin of pride. The erratic impulse to constantly try and do the decent thing that keeps breaking through will really be the death of you one of these days."

When he went out to the courtyard there was no sign of Kleiber and Sindermann or the Embassy car. The porter emerged from the lodge.

"Can I be of service, General?"

"Sturmbannführer Kleiber. Have you seen any sign of him?"

"He hasn't returned yet. His driver did phone in some time ago to say they were at the Club Flamenco. Apparently the Sturmbannführer is waiting for someone."

Schellenberg cursed softly. "Get me a car," he said. "And make it quick."

When Connie and the boys entered the Club Flamenco, the place was deserted. No sign of anyone, not even the caretaker, but Billy Joe's guitar and double bass were arranged neatly on the small stage beside Harry Gray's drums.

"Hey, somebody unpacked for us," Billy Joe said. "I call that real friendly."

The curtain behind the stage parted and Kleiber stepped through. "That was me. I admire order; in all things."

Sindermann moved around from behind the

door, blocking the way to the outside. Connie glanced over his shoulder at him, then back to Kleiber.

"What is this?"

"I'll tell you," Kleiber said. "I have a feeling you've been playing games with me, you black ape. I think you know where Hannah Winter is. I think she may even be here."

"We're not in Nazi land now," Connie said. "Why don't you go fuck yourself?"

Sindermann moved in very fast and punched him in the spine, putting Connie on his knees.

"Expensive this, eh?" Kleiber indicated the double bass.

He stamped hard, snapping it in two, then put his foot through the large drum. Billy Joe and Harry cried out in anger and started forward, and he drew a Luger from his coat pocket to menace them.

"Come on. Try it. I'd like nothing better than a chance to rid the world of such vermin."

They stayed where they were, crouched, watching, and he called to Sindermann, "Make him talk, Gunter."

Connie was still on his knees, and Sindermann moved in and kicked him at the base of the spine. Connie fell flat on his face, and Sindermann picked him up and threw him casually against the bar.

He was enjoying himself now, and he flexed his huge arms slowly, then moved close and hoisted Connie across the bar.

"Speak up, ape," he said softly, rubbing himself against Connie, leaning hard. "You like that, don't you," he whispered in his ear, the excitement rising in him.

"He plays the piano for a living, Gunter. How would he manage without a few fingers?"

Connie was half-unconscious. Sindermann grinned and, holding the Negro's right hand flat on the bar, leaned across and took a full bottle of brandy from the shelf, gripping it by the neck.

He had raised it like a hammer poised to strike when a quiet voice said, "Enough, Sindermann. Now let him go."

Sindermann turned his head slowly. His face was bathed with sweat, and there was a vacant look in his eyes.

Kleiber said, "General, these men have information of the greatest importance."

"These men, as you term them, are American citizens in a neutral country, and you, Kleiber, are promoting an incident which in the international press could do the Reich nothing but harm."

"General Schellenberg, I must protest."

"Get your feet together when you speak to me, Sturmbannführer, and put that gun away."

Kleiber did as he was told; slowly, but he did it. "You want to play games, we'll play games," Schellenberg said. "You swore an oath on joining the SS, am I right? A holy oath. Repeat it now."

Kleiber stared rigidly ahead as he spoke. "I swear to you Adolf Hitler as Führer and Chancellor of the German Reich, loyalty and courage. I vow to you and the superiors appointed by you, obedience unto death, so help me God."

"You would agree that I am your superior officer, appointed by the Führer?"

"Yes, Brigadeführer."

"So, remember in future, you do as you're told." His voice was very cold now. "If I ask you a question, you will answer, *Jawohl, Brigadeführer*. If I give you an order, it's heels together and *Zu Befehl, Brigadeführer*. Do you understand?"

"Jawohl, Brigadeführer."

"Good." Schellenberg turned to Sindermann. "Put him down and stand to attention."

But Sindermann had gone beyond the point of reason now. "No!" he said.

"I could shoot you," Schellenberg told him. "But we haven't got much time, so I'll content myself with teaching you a lesson instead. When I look at you, you fill me with disgust. What are you, after all? About 250 pounds of bone and muscle. Brute force, and what good is that with a mind the size of a pea?"

Sindermann dropped Connie and charged, arms raised to destroy. Schellenberg pivoted to one side and delivered a left to Sindermann's kidneys as he lurched past. Sindermann fell to one knee, and Schellenberg picked up a chair and smashed it across his back. Then he stood and waited.

As Sindermann got up and swung a wild punch, Schellenberg sank a left under his ribs, followed by a right hook that landed on the cheek, splitting flesh.

"I'm afraid I haven't been honest with you, Sturmscharführer. When I was first asked to join the SS, I pointed out that I wasn't a particularly physical specimen. But that didn't matter, my superiors said. It was my intelligence they were after, something you would know nothing about. Learning how to fight is easy, you can teach anyone."

He punched Sindermann in the face again and kicked him under the right kneecap. "Especially how to fight dirty."

Sindermann went down and stayed on his knees, sobbing. Schellenberg said, "Next time, I kill you. Understand?"

Sindermann's voice was low, but his reply was quite clear. "Jawohl, Brigadeführer."

"Good." Schellenberg turned to Kleiber. "Get the driver to give you a hand with him to the car and let's get moving. The pilot will be wondering what's happened."

Kleiber did as he was told. Billy Joe had Connie in a chair at one of the tables and Harry brought brandy from the bar.

"He may need a doctor," Schellenberg said. "He could have cracked a couple of ribs."

Billy Joe shook his head. "Man, I can't figure you out, but thanks anyway."

Kleiber and the driver had assisted Sindermann out between them, and Schellenberg started toward the door. He paused and turned to face them.

"Just for the record, a matter of personal interest entirely. She did make it? She is on her way to Lisbon? Am I right?"

Connie opened his mouth and said hoarsely, "General, why don't you . . ."

Schellenberg smiled. "Thank you, Mister Jones, for answering my question."

The door closed softly behind him.

NINE

THE DUKE OF WINDSOR had been closeted with the British Ambassador, Sir Walford Selby, for more than an hour, and the Duchess was in the lower garden cutting roses when he found her. She knew that telegrams had been flying back and forth between her husband and Winston Churchill for some days now. He had even sent Major Gray Phillips of the Black Watch, who had been acting as their household comptroller, to London to speak personally for him to the Prime Minister, in the hope that a more important post might be found.

"How did it go, David?"

"Not so good. Winston's latest message seems quite final. So, the Bahamas it is."

"I see. Well, if we must go, we must go, I suppose."

There was a call and their host, Dr. Ricardo de Espirito Santo é Silva, leaned over the balustrade.

"Your Royal Highness has a visitor. The Marqués de Estella. I've put him in the library."

"You go, David," she said. "I still need a few more flowers. I'll see you on the terrace for tea."

She sat beside the pool for almost an hour, and there was still no sign of the Duke and Primo de Rivera. Finally, she heard voices in the courtyard at the other end of the terrace. When she went and looked over she was just in time to see De Rivera getting into his car. The Duke waved goodbye and came up the steps.

"What happened?" she demanded.

"Oh, he has some evening function at the Spanish Embassy tonight. Had to get off. Sent his apologies." They walked along the terrace, his arm around her shoulder. "You know, Wallis, this whole business is beginning to assume rather farcical elements."

As they sat down a manservant brought fresh tea. "What do you mean?"

"I hear from De Rivera that the wicked British Secret Service would like to get their hands on me, according to Madrid society gossip at the moment."

"Oh, David, what nonsense."

"Well, the logic behind it is really quite simple. It's common knowledge I'm not too happy about the Bahamas appointment, and many people seem to think it a distinct possibility that I might refuse to go. Stay here in Portugal or Spain instead. Now, that wouldn't look too good from the British government's point of view."

"So they send the Secret Service to drag you off to the Bahamas by the scruff of the neck? How absurd."

"De Rivera seemed more concerned about the possibility that I wouldn't get there at all. Over the rail one dark night and so on."

"That's terrible. How could he think such a thing?"

"Now, Wallis, you must admit I've been a considerable nuisance in certain people's eyes for quite some time now." He was teasing her and she knew it.

"I don't like it, David, this sort of talk. It isn't funny, not after France. I'll never forget that." She shivered. "I'm not even sure that I like this place any more. Too many policemen around."

"Well, we're going to change all that. You shall have an outing. A day in the country. De Rivera has a friend who owns a bull farm. You know what I mean? Fighting bulls for the ring. He says they'll stage a couple of fights for us and we can look the place over, have a picnic. That sort of thing. How does it sound to you?"

"Marvelous."

"Good." He smiled. "Let's go in now. Getting a little chilly and I smell rain on the wind."

The Police Attaché at the German Legation was named Egger and only too happy to assist in any way he was able when Kleiber was introduced to him.

"How may I be of service, Sturmbannführer?"

"How good are your relations with the police here?"

"Excellent," Egger told him. "There is a considerable amount of political sympathy for the ideals of National Socialism in Portugal at the moment."

"There's a possibility that this woman could turn up here in Lisbon at any time. Here's her description."

He pushed a sheet across with a photo of Hannah pinned to it. "Hannah Winter," Egger said. "What has she done?"

"Shot three security men dead in Berlin, so we want her very badly indeed."

"She is a citizen of the Reich?"

"Of course," Kleiber said, "but she's been using an American passport."

"That won't do her any good here. Not once I

communicate these facts to the Security Police. They mount a guard on all foreign embassies. You must have noticed it on your way in here. If she tries to approach the American Embassy, they'll have her—as soon as I've given them these details, that is."

As he reached for the phone, Kleiber said, "By the way, the Duke of Windsor at Estoril. I don't suppose anyone can get in to see him without passing through the Security Police also."

"So I understand," Egger said.

"Good. My thanks." Kleiber got up. "I'll see you again, I'm sure, while I'm here."

Sindermann was waiting for him in the anteroom. He had a black eye, his right cheek badly swollen and criss-crossed with adhesive where the flesh had split.

"Is everything in order, Sturmbannführer?"

"Fine, Gunter. Couldn't be better. The Portuguese Security Police are on the job now. The moment she shows her face, she's ours. Where's the General?"

"With the Ambassador. They've booked us rooms at a hotel just around the corner that most of the Legation staff use."

"Good, then let's go and see what it's like. I'm hungry."

* * *

Baron Oswald von Hoyningen-Huene, Minister to the German Legation in Lisbon, was a very different man from Von Stohrer, his Madrid counterpart. He was a genuine aristocrat, a man of considerable culture and refinement. He was also, as Schellenberg well knew, no Nazi. In fact, it was a standing joke in the Diplomatic Service that the legation in Lisbon was staffed by a considerable number of people who saw it as an easy jumping-off point to America if the day came when their lack of political conviction caught up with them.

Huene examined the Führer order which Schellenberg passed to him. "Naturally, I shall give you every assistance I can in his matter, General. The terms of the Führer's letter give me no choice."

"Which means that you don't approve of this whole affair," Schellenberg said.

Huene sat there, staring at him calmly for a moment. "General Schellenberg, what exactly are you trying to say to me?"

"That I don't think much of the idea myself. It's nonsense. There, I've said it, Baron. What happens now? Do you pick up the telephone and place a call to Reichsminister Ribbentrop?"

"No," Huene said. "What I do is get a bottle of the cognac I keep in the cabinet over there and two glasses and we talk, completely off the record, of course."

Schellenberg sampled the cognac. "Excellent; but to the Windsor affair. Do you honestly think the Duke is on our side in the present European situation?"

"Frankly, no," said Huene. "Oh, he's not happy about this Bahamas posting they've given him. He'd hoped for more and he's made no secret of the fact and he is, I think, very bitter at what he sees as a continuing vendetta against him by certain elements in British society. He's certainly pro-German, but with his family background one would expect that."

"Which is a very different thing from being in favor of National Socialism."

"Exactly." Huene shook his head. "No, if Ribbentrop and the Führer think differently, then they're much mistaken." He poured Schellenberg another cognac. "So—where does that leave you, General? With only one choice, as I see it."

"Abduction?" Schellenberg shook his head. "I don't think so. In my opinion, there would be nothing to be gained by such an action and it would be greatly to our discredit internationally. If I am wrong; if the Duke indicates a desire to go to Spain of his own volition, then I shall give him every assistance in the matter. But otherwise . . ."

"Good. I'm glad we are in accord on this thing,"
Huene said. "I have to work here, remember. It's
a constant battle for influence with the Portuguese between us and the British. The abduction
of the Duke would hardly redound to our credit,
however much the present government is in
sympathy with us." He stood up. "Will you have
dinner with me tonight?"

"Another time, if I may," Schellenberg said.
"I've people to see. Old friends. What about ac-
commodations?"

"There's a place around the corner where
many of the staff live permanently. Rooms have
been booked there for yourself and your two Gestapo associates. I've also provided a car and a
driver for your personal use. A Buick."

"Frankly, I should prefer somewhere different
to stay."

"I know a place, not too far away, kept by a
Dutch-Jewish family. Quiet and very comfortable and the food is excellent. Duisenberg, the
people are called."

Schellenberg said, "Then if you'll be kind
enough to give them a ring, I'll get the driver to
take me there now."

Just before the Madrid-Lisbon Express crossed
into Portugal at Valencia al Cantara, Hannah
threw the Walther pistol out of the toilet window

in case of a body search by customs. There was an inspection on the Portuguese side at Marvão. She was carrying only a small suitcase that Connie had given her. He and the boys had filled it with an assortment of towels, toilet articles, and a few items purchased at the station kiosk in Madrid.

She used the French passport and explained her lack of luggage by telling the customs officer that her theatrical trunk was coming later by freight train. There was no difficulty—no difficulty at all—and she slept for the rest of the journey, arriving in Lisbon later than expected because of a lengthy delay near Ponte de Sor. It was after eight o'clock when she walked out of the station and approached the cab rank.

At her third attempt, she found a driver who spoke some English. "You know the villa of Dr. Ricardo de Espirito Santo é Silva in Estoril?"

"Yes, senhorita."

"Take me there."

God, but she was tired—so very, very tired. She leaned back against the seat and closed her eyes.

She came awake quite suddenly as the car braked to a halt. They had stopped outside an ironwork gate set in a high wall. A policeman was standing beside it, a carbine over one shoul-

der, and he sauntered forward and leaned down
and spoke to the driver in Portuguese.

The driver turned. "He'd like to know what
you want, senhorita?"

"To see the Duke of Windsor."

"And now your papers."

She produced her own passport and passed it
across. The policeman took it to the gate and put
it through the bars to a sergeant who had
emerged from a small lodge. He, too, examined
it then went inside. After a few minutes he came
out again and passed the passport back through
the bars to the first policeman, who returned it
to Hannah.

"Can I go in now?" she demanded eagerly.

There was a further conversation in Portuguese and the cab driver said, "I'm afraid not,
senhorita. They have a special concern for the
Duke's safety. No visitors are allowed through
without the permission of police headquarters.
He has made the necessary telephone call. Now
he must wait for a reply."

"I see."

"Shall I stay, senhorita?"

"No—I don't think so. I could do with some
fresh air."

She paid him off and he drove away. Through
the trees, she could see lights in the villa and

there was the sound of music. She walked some little way up the road, turned, and came back again.

Just after midnight, it started to rain and the young Portuguese policeman, the one who could speak no English, brought a cape from his sentry box and placed it around her shoulders without a word.

It was quite cold now and she walked a few paces along the road to keep warm, pausing to look back across the mouth of the Tagus to where the lights of Lisbon gleamed in the distance.

A long way; not as far as Berlin or Paris, but she was here now, finally, outside the pink stucco villa at Estoril. The final end of things, more tired than she had ever been in her life before, and suddenly she wanted it to be over.

She turned and walked back to the policeman. "Please," she said in English. "How much longer? I've been here almost an hour."

Which was foolish because he didn't understand her. At that moment, there was the sound of a car coming up the hill, headlights flashed across the mimosa bushes and a black Mercedes braked to a halt a few yards away.

* * *

Rain swept in across the Tagus and rattled the window of Joe Jackson's apartment as he threw another log on the fire.

"That's really quite a story. Will you excuse me for a minute? I'll be right back. Help yourself to another drink."

She poured a little more brandy into her glass and sat there in front of the fire, nursing the glass between her hands, staring into the flames.

As he returned, she glanced up. "Do you believe me?"

"Those guys on the wharf, Kleiber and Sindermann? Let's just say I like you and I don't like them. That's as good a starting point as any. And the Duke of Windsor is up there in Santo é Silva's villa at Estoril. That's a fact."

"But we must get to him somehow, don't you see that?" she said urgently. "We can't just stand by and let the Nazis take him. Not you especially. You fought against them in the International Brigade. Connie told me."

"He should also have mentioned that these days I'm strictly a neutral, angel. Abyssinia, Spain—other men's wars. I've had a bellyful, believe me. At the moment, I run a nice quiet bar and that's enough."

"For a man like you? I don't believe it." She stood up. "Anyway, if you won't help me, I'll go to the American Embassy or the British."

"And get picked up by the Portuguese police trying to get in? They now have an extradition warrant for your arrest for no less than three murders, and the Portuguese government is pursuing a policy of friendly cooperation with Germany at the moment, remember."

"I'll tell them my story, then. They'll have to do something."

"Why should they? They're already mounting a strong guard on the villa, and it all sounds pretty wild, you've got to admit that. The invention of a very frightened young woman who'd say anything rather than be sent back to Germany, where she'd certainly face the headsman. Did you know they make you lie face upward on the block so you see the axe descend? They think of everything, Himmler and friends, you've got to give them that."

She sat there, staring up at him. "What can I do? How can I make you believe me?"

The telephone started to ring in the next room. "You can't, but Connie Jones might be able to. That'll be him now. I placed a call through to the Flamenco in Madrid."

He smiled slightly, went out, and closed the door. She could hear the murmur of his voice for quite some time. Finally, he returned.

He grinned and spread his arms slightly. "So, it's all true. On top of that, according to Connie, you can sing like Billie Holiday. I give in. He'd like a word with you."

She hurried into the other room, and Jackson lit a cigarette and stood frowning down into the fire. She was gone for quite some time and when she returned she looked as if she'd been crying.

"Did he tell you about what happened at the club?" she said.

"Sure. Three cracked ribs, but he told me it hadn't affected his playing. They've managed to borrow instruments for the time being. Don't worry, I'll have some new drums and a bass waiting for them when they get here next week."

"But Schellenberg?" she whispered. "Why did he do what he did? I just don't understand him?"

"Yes, I thought that was one of the more improbable parts of your story—the way he helped you escape in Berlin. I mean, the guy was really putting his head on the block when he did that."

"Then why?"

"I don't know. Maybe he doesn't even know why himself—maybe he just liked you, angel." He smiled. "That's not hard to understand. But never mind that now. We've got to get you out of here, just in case those goons come back."

"And the Portuguese police?" she said. "What if they do decide to bring them into it?"

"Ah, I can handle that." He smiled crookedly. "Some of my best friends are policemen, especially the variety who patronize the downstairs gaming room. They seem to win pretty regularly, you see, so everybody is happy. Now get your coat and let's move."

In 1938, one of Schellenberg's first pieces of active espionage had involved a visit to Dakar, to obtain as much information as possible about what was then the chief French naval station in Africa.

Most of his preparations for the task had taken place in Lisbon, where he had been introduced to a Japanese businessman, Kajiro Taniguchi. A genuine friendship had developed between the two men, and Taniguchi had been able to assist Schellenberg in many ways with the African adventure. He seemed to have a finger in all sorts of schemes, had close contacts with the local criminal fraternity, and Schellenberg had long ago decided that he was probably an agent of the Japanese government.

He tried phoning Taniguchi at home and was told by a servant that he was still at his place of business, an import-export agency on the Alcantara Docks. Schellenberg drove there himself in the Buick provided by the Legation, having told the driver who had been supplied, to take the night off. In these circumstances he much preferred to be on his own.

The offices themselves were in darkness when
he got there, but when he drove into the yard of
the warehouse adjacent, there was a light at an
upper window. He parked the car and crossed to
the warehouse door.

As he opened it, a voice called in Portuguese,
"Who's there?"

The warehouse was crammed with bales and
boxes of every description. High above was a
glass-walled office reached by an iron staircase,
and Kajiro Taniguchi stood at the top of it, a
mountain of a man, built like a Sumo wrestler.

He peered down into the shadows and then a
delighted smile appeared on his face. "Walter—
Walter Schellenberg," he said in English, for he
spoke little German, "by all that's holy."

"Business, Walter, it must always be so with
you, I think?"

Schellenberg said, "The Duke of Windsor is
staying at Santo é Silva's villa near Estoril."

"Common knowledge," Taniguchi said. "I saw
the Duke and Duchess myself only two nights
ago, dining at a well-known restaurant in the
city."

"I want to know everything there is to know
about that villa. The layout of the place, the servant situation. Just how good the security is and
so on. To have someone in the house itself, of

course, to keep me posted as to comings and goings would be marvelous. I should stress that money is no object in this matter. I have unlimited funds. We can afford to pay very highly indeed for any useful information received."

He paused, waiting. Taniguchi said, "Have another saki. It really is quite delicious."

"Can you handle it?"

"But of course," Taniguchi said tranquilly. "I know everyone, Walter—everyone in this town who matters, and in Lisbon money talks very loudly indeed, believe me."

"When will you have something for me?"

"Tomorrow afternoon. Let's say two o'clock. But now, my friend, what of you? A general now, I hear. A major general at thirty. Remarkable."

"I've been lucky."

"But are you happy, Walter?"

"Happy?" Schellenberg said. "I don't even know what the word means. How do you define it? How do you find happiness?"

"By not looking for it. By sitting still, without going outside, you may know the whole world. Without looking through the window, you may see the ways of heaven. The farther we go, the less we know."

"More of your Japanese philosophy?"

"Chinese, actually. You think you are going

to win the war?" he asked with an abrupt change of direction.

"Let's look at the facts," Schellenberg said. "We control more of Europe than Napoleon did; most neutral countries left tend to sympathize with our point of view and America, let's face it, doesn't want to know. Our sources in London indicate that the American Ambassador there, Joseph Kennedy, believes a German victory is certain and is considering resigning."

"So, you think the Panzers will soon be driving along the Mall to Buckingham Palace?"

"It's up to the British. The Führer made it perfectly clear he's willing to settle for an Armistice. Of course, they may want to do it the hard way. For some perverse reason, they usually do."

"Another theme of ancient Chinese wisdom," Taniguchi said. "If men are not afraid to die, it is of no avail to threaten them."

Schellenberg got up. "I must be off. I'll be in touch tomorrow."

He went down the staircase. Taniguchi called softly, "My poor Walter, there is always an official executioner. What a pity it has to be you." Then he went back into his office.

TEN

THE AGENT known in Abwehr files as A-1416, and discussed by Canaris and Schellenberg during their walk in the Tiergarten, was a German industrialist named Erich Becker, now a naturalized Portuguese citizen. He had wide business interests which enabled him to cover a lot of territory and lived well on the profits, inflated by contributions not only from the Abwehr, but also from British Intelligence. He had a superb apartment near the Jeronimos monastery with views down to the Tagus.

He was unmarried, which left him free to amuse himself with a wide variety of women. In fact, he was entertaining one in bed when his doorbell rang. He tried to ignore it, but whoever it was simply wouldn't go away. He pulled on a robe and leaned over to kiss the girl who sprawled there in his bed, her long blonde hair spread across the pillow.

"I won't be long, my sweet," he said.

He opened the door on the chain. "Who in the hell is it? Don't you know what time it is?"

"Yes, ten minutes past midnight," Walter Schellenberg said.

Becker's mouth gaped in astonishment. "My God—you!" He got the door open quickly.

Schellenberg glanced around the room. "You are doing well for yourself these days."

Becker went to the bedroom door and closed it. "It's—it's good to see you again, General."

"I was talking about you with Admiral Canaris the other day. Told him I was coming to Lisbon, so he suggested I get in touch with you if I needed assistance. He did signal you to that effect, did he not?"

Becker smiled nervously. "I'm afraid you have me at a loss."

"The Windsor affair? The reason I'm here? Admiral Canaris told you all about it in that nice long signal he sent you, didn't he?"

"I'm sorry, General," Becker said, "but I really don't know what you're talking about."

Schellenberg's hand emerged from his right hand pocket holding the Mauser; it coughed once, and a rather pretty China dog on the coffee table at the other end of the room disintegrated.

"Good, aren't they?" he said pleasantly. "Handguns are usually such nasty loud things, whereas if I shot you in each kneecap with this, the only thing the young lady you undoubtedly have in bed in the next room would hear would be your screams."

Becker sweating, said, "What do you want from me?"

"The truth," Schellenberg said. "You received a signal from Admiral Canaris telling you I'd be in town and why, didn't you?"

"Yes, I heard this morning."

"And what were your instructions?"

"To keep an eye on you. Report back on your activities."

Schellenberg almost laughed out loud. What an old fox Canaris was.

Becker said, "I need a drink." He walked over to a cupboard in rosewood, with an intricate Moorish design inset in brass, and opened it. "Whiskey all right for you?"

"You know in Abwehr files you're known as A-1416. Were you aware of that?"

"Yes," Becker said.

"Typically German," Schellenberg told him. "To reduce a man to a number on a file—our greatest failing. The English, on the other hand,

are much more imaginative. Hamlet—I like
that. What a perfect name for a double agent.
To be or not to be."

Becker stood staring at him, a tumbler of
whiskey in each hand, despair on his face.
"That's right," Schellenberg said. "The jig's up,
so let's be sensible. You did pass on to our English friends the information you received in
that signal from the Admiral? That I was on
my way and why? Am I right?"

"Yes," Becker whispered and emptied one of
the tumblers of whiskey.

"Yes, I thought you would and so did the
Admiral. Does that surprise you? The only reason you've survived this long is because he
found you useful to shovel false information
across to your friends in London. Of course, on
this occasion, the information is a hundred per-
cent correct, mainly because, like a lot of people,
he can't make his mind up which side he's on."

Becker gulped down the contents of the other
tumbler. "What are you going to do with me?"

"That depends how sensible you are. Who's
your contact with British Intelligence?"

"A Major Frear."

"Here in Lisbon?"

"Yes."

Schellenberg put the Mauser back in his

pocket and lit a cigarette. "Get him on the telephone. Tell him I'm here."

Becker looked bewildered. "But why?"

Schellenberg stood there, hands in the pockets of his open leather trench coat, the cigarette drooping from the corner of his mouth.

"Well, I *am* here, which is an indisputable fact he'll discover for himself, sooner or later. If you tell him first, he'll be inclined to believe anything else you tell him later, which could be rather useful to me."

Becker hesitated, then shrugged, went to the dark rosewood desk at the other end of the room, sat down behind it, and reached for the telephone. At the same time he slipped open a drawer on his right and took out a revolver.

"And now, General!" he said.

Schellenberg, the Mauser ready in his right hand under the trench coat, shot him twice in the heart. Becker went over backward with a crash, taking the chair with him.

Schellenberg waited, facing the bedroom door, but there was no sound. He walked around the desk and looked down at Becker. The holes in the bathrobe over the heart covered no more than the width of two fingers. There was very little blood.

"If you intend to kill a man, do it, don't start

making speeches," he said softly. "You learned
that too late, didn't you, my friend?"

He let himself out, closing the door softly behind him. In the bedroom, the young blonde
stirred in her sleep, reached out, and found
nothing there.

"Erich?" she called, "come back to bed." Then
she turned, cradling the pillow, and slept
again.

The run along the coast road in Joe Jackson's
Mercedes sports car seemed to be taking them
back toward Estoril and Hannah said, "Where
are we going?"

"A fishing village named Cascais," Jackson
told her. "A friend of mine has a house just
outside, near the beach in a pine wood. Nice
and quiet and secluded. She's away at the moment, but I've got the key."

"She won't mind?"

"I shouldn't think so."

It was a fine night now, the rain long gone,
and there was a full moon in a clear sky. Far
out to sea, dozens of lights bobbed in toward the
harbor of the small village down below.

"Lanterns on the prows of the fishing boats,"
he said. "It attracts the fish in great shoals,
rather like moths to a flame. An interesting
place, Cascais. It was a fisherman from here

who discovered America ten years before Columbus."

"I don't believe you."

"True. He was called Afonso Sanches, and during a voyage to the East Indies his boat was carried off to the coast of America by contrary winds in a great storm. He finally made it back to Madeira with a few companions, all in a terrible state. Columbus was living in Madeira at the time and got hold of Sanches' log."

"It's a good story," she said.

"I wouldn't scoff at it in Cascais, if I were you. They take it very seriously here."

They were close to a wide beach with sand dunes backed by pine trees, and he swung the car into a narrow track, finally halting at a gate in white walls. He got out and unlocked it, then got back into the Mercedes, and they drove through into an enclosed courtyard.

The house was single story with a red pantile roof and a veranda, L-shaped and surrounded by a garden; she was aware of that because of the perfume of mimosa on the night air.

He unlocked the front door, switched on the light, and led the way into an enormous living room which was furnished with startling simplicity: white-painted walls, a huge stone fireplace, the wooden floor polished and scattered with oriental rugs.

"Bathroom, kitchen. Bedroom—the only one. The room in the other part of the house is a studio. Lots of canvases around and so on, so I'd stay out of there if I were you. Plenty of canned food in the kitchen. I'll be back tomorrow with a few other things. If you'd like to make some coffee, I'll light a fire for you, then I'll get back."

She did as she was told. When she finally returned to the living room, a log fire burned brightly on the hearth. The door was open and Joe Jackson was standing on the veranda. Somewhere in the distance, she heard music, sad and strangely exciting.

"What is it?" she asked as she gave him his coffee.

"Local café. Somebody's playing a *fado* record."

"*Fado*—what's that?"

"Can't be explained, only experienced. Part of the Portuguese way of life. I'll take you to hear some one night."

The trees around were heavy with olives. She could smell them in the night. There was something quite incredible in the realization that two nights before she had been in Berlin and now, here she was on the most westerly edge of Europe, facing out into the Atlantic to America, three thousand miles away.

"So, what happens now?"

"You get a good night's sleep and leave the rest to me."

She put a hand on his arm. "You will do something, won't you? Promise me?"

"Sure, I will. Look, we can't go marching you in personally, not with this extradition thing hanging over your head. I'll see your story gets to the right people myself."

"When?"

"Tonight—in Lisbon. I think I know the man to speak to."

She stood there, staring up at him, and suddenly kissed him on the cheek. Then she went in without a word. Jackson stayed there for quite some time after the door closed, before turning and going back to the car.

Without doubt, the most beautiful district of the city of Lisbon is Alfama. The high walls of the Castelo de São Jorge tower above it, in whose moats swim swans, ducks, and flamingos.

Below is the old Alfama quarter, and Joe Jackson parked the Mercedes and plunged into the maze of narrow alleys, most of them wide enough to allow two donkeys to pass and no more.

Usually it was like a rabbit warren, teeming with the rich life of the old city, but at that time

in the morning it was silent, a place of shadows
with the occasional pool of light on some street
corner from huge iron lanterns bracketed high
on the ancient walls.

Below, through narrow openings, he caught
a glimpse of the Tagus, the lights of the docks.
There was a freighter in mid-channel moving
out to sea.

Finally, he turned into a square at the back
of the cathedral and paused outside what, in
other days, had been a nobleman's house. There
was a coat of arms set in stone above the archway, and the oaken door was very old and bound
in iron.

He pulled on a bell chain. After a while, a
small gate opened. It closed instantly, a bolt
was withdrawn, and the door opened. A small,
dark-haired man in white tuxedo stood back to
let him in.

"Senhor Joe—a pleasure," he said in Portuguese.

"Hello, Tomas."

Jackson walked through into an enclosed
courtyard, floored with Moorish tiles. A fountain played in the center. He followed Tomas
across and through an archway into a comfortable little bar.

There were a number of small tables, and the
girls sitting at them waiting for customers lived

up to the elegant atmosphere. They were simply beautiful women, elegantly dressed.

"I heard there was a big game on tonight in number four."

Tomas nodded. "Stud poker."

"Then Major Frear must be sitting in on it, sweating as usual."

"Yes—for two hours now."

"Tell him I'd like to see him."

"He won't like it, Senhor Joe. I believe he's heavily into a winning streak."

"I'll be on the terrace," Jackson said. "If he's not down in five minutes, I'll come and get him."

Tomas shrugged and went out. Jackson said to the blonde girl behind the bar, "Champagne for the ladies and bring me the usual."

He opened the French windows and went outside. The vine-covered terrace offered a spectacular view of the river, lights gleaming down there in the darkness below the Alfama rooftops. The bar girl brought him brandy and soda with crushed ice in a heavy crystal glass, and he leaned on the balcony, wondering suddenly what he was doing here.

Joe Jackson was thirty years of age. Son of a Methodist minister, the greatest influence on his life had been his mother's brother, Grant Hayward, who'd flown with the Lafayette Escadrille in France during the First World War.

The boy had been raised on talk of Spads and Fokkers, and his heroes were Von Richtofen, Rickenbacker, Bishop, and Mannock.

By the age of twelve, he knew that you never crossed the line alone under ten thousand feet and watched the sun constantly. He first soloed at sixteen, thanks to his uncle's weekend lessons, and disappointed his father at nineteen by dropping out of Harvard after one year and joining the Air Corps.

He had trained as a fighter pilot, but the discipline of service life irked him, and in 1933 he had resigned and taken a job flying mail in Brazil.

For a while he had worked out of Djibouti in French Somaliland, ferrying arms to Addis Ababa during Mussolini's Ethiopian campaign, flying Dakotas over some of the worst country in the world.

And then Spain, where he had at last been able to put into operation those lessons learned at Uncle Grant's knee all those years before. The only snag had been that, in his case, he'd been given a Bristol fighter to fly, a biplane of First World War vintage: an excellent aircraft in its day, but the German pilots of the Condor Legion had the new Messerschmitt Bf-109s.

He shot down a 109, an Arado biplane, and three Fiat fighters, a score of five, which officially made him an ace, before he was blasted out of the sky over Barcelona one fine April morning by the German ace, Werner Molders.

Afterward, because of the acute shortage of aircraft in the closing stages of the war, he had served on the ground as adjutant to Frank Ryan, the great I.R.A. leader, who was at that time acting brigadier in the Abraham Lincoln Brigade. He had missed the final debacle of the Civil War, thanks to a bullet in the chest, which had brought him finally to Lisbon to convalesce.

He had stayed and prospered. Stayed longer than he had stayed anywhere before. There were mornings he watched the Clipper take off from the Tagus, America its eventual destination, and wished with all his heart that he was on board, but by the evening...

There was a quick step behind, and he turned as Frear came in. He wore a crumpled white linen suit and a Guards tie. His hair and mustache were snow white, and he seemed at least sixty when, to Jackson's knowledge, he was ten years younger. Just now he also looked petulant and annoyed.

"What in the hell is this all about, Joseph? I'm in the middle of the best run I've had in months, and I don't like being taken away from it, I can tell you."

Frear was a compulsive gambler, his sole

vice. He was also an agent for MI-6, that branch of the British Secret Service concerned with espionage in foreign countries.

Jackson said, "The Duke of Windsor. Were you aware that the Germans have more than a passing interest in him?"

"Good God, Joseph, is that all? Rumors flying around Lisbon ever since His Royal Highness arrived. Load of cobblers. If that's the best you can do, I'll get back to my game."

"Suit yourself," Jackson said. "Only earlier tonight I ran into a young woman just in from Berlin who had something rather more concrete to offer."

Frear came back. "Name of Winter? Hannah Winter?"

"That's right."

Frear sighed, turned, and called, "A large Scotch and soda, sweetheart, and the same again for Mr. Jackson."

Jackson said, "How did you know?"

"My dear Joseph, I pay a certain lieutenant of police at General Headquarters a handsome weekly stipend to phone me at precisely nine o'clock each evening to convey any information worth having concerning the day's events. This evening he tells me that top of the list on every police blotter in Lisbon is a young German woman named Hannah Winter, wanted for murder in Berlin. Extradition warrant served apparently."

"American," Jackson said. "Not German— that's if you're interested. If you call rubbing out three Gestapo hit men murder, then she's certainly guilty of that, but that isn't the reason they've chased her across Europe to Lisbon. It's because a man called Walter Schellenberg's in town, and she knows why."

Frear's smile stayed firmly in place, but the expression in his eyes had changed. The bar girl brought the drinks on a tray, turned, and went out again.

"Lovely arse on her, that girl." Frear sipped his Scotch. "Walter Schellenberg here? I mean actually here? You sure, old boy?"

"Why, do you know him?"

"Yes, I think you could say that. All right, Joseph, tell me what the young lady has to say."

ELEVEN

WINSTON CHURCHILL became Prime Minister on May 10, 1940, and continued for some weeks to live and work at Admiralty House in the rooms he had occupied as First Lord of the Admiralty.

That evening, a meeting with the Joint Chiefs of Staff, concerned with what at that time seemed the imminent possibility of a German invasion, had dragged on until after midnight. He had retired shortly after, falling asleep instantly, a trick learned the hard way during the numerous campaigns of his youth.

He was awakened at 2 A.M. by Alexander Cadogan, Head of the Foreign Office.

"Now what?" the Prime Minister demanded,

adding with a touch of that black humor for which he was famous, "Don't tell me, let me guess. Eight thousand Fallschirmjäger of the Seventh Fliegerdivision have dropped around Hythe and Dymchurch and secured a bridgehead. I can conceive of no other reason why you should wake me at this hour."

"No, Prime Minister, but two signals have been received from Lisbon from our MI-6 station in the city. They have in their employ a double agent, code name Hamlet, who also works for the Abwehr. The second signal would seem to confirm his story."

The Prime Minister propped himself up against the pillows and lit a cigar, then held out his hand for the signals. He read them, then sat there in silence for quite some time.

"Prime Minister?" Cadogan said finally. "What do you think?"

"The suggestion that His Royal Highness might actually deal with our enemies, I treat with the contempt it deserves. I have known him all his life and he is a man of finest honor." Here Churchill scowled. "Indeed, if I may say so, in that fact is to be found the cause of much of his trouble during that most distressing period of his life."

"But the other aspect, Prime Minister? The possibility of his abduction? General Schellenberg's presence in Lisbon can only constitute the gravest of threats."

"The Portuguese dictator, Salazar, may lean more in his political sympathies toward the Nazis than to ourselves, but he could never tolerate such an overt act of aggression on his own soil. The international repercussions would be tremendous."

"Then what do we do?"

"The British Ambassador must make our fears plain at the highest level possible in the Portuguese Government. Not officially, but informally, I think that's the way to play it at the moment. He must also inform His Royal Highness of the situation."

"And then?"

"We pack him off to the Bahamas as soon as possible. Find out the first available boat, and get hold of Walter Monckton for me."

Walter Monckton, roused from his bed, arrived at Admiralty House just after 3 A.M. and was shown straight in to the Prime Minister.

Walter Turner Monckton was of medium height with thinning hair and thick glasses. A brilliant barrister and friend of the Duke of Windsor when they were at Oxford together, he had been his most valued aide during the Abdication Crisis. In the years that followed, he had remained the British Government's emissary to the Duke in time of need. He was at the present moment Director General of the Ministry of Information.

"Walter," the Prime Minister said. "I want you to go to Lisbon as soon as a flight may be arranged. Our understanding is that there is an American ship leaving for Bermuda on the first of August. I wish you to use your best offices to see that His Royal Highness and the Duchess are on board."

"And if he will not, Prime Minister?"

"He must, Walter. Look at these signals and judge for yourself."

Monckton read them through, his face calm as always, then handed them back.

"You will do this for me, Walter?"

"Of course, Prime Minister." Monckton hesitated. "Is His Majesty aware of the situation?"

"Not at the moment, and I see no cause to alarm him unnecessarily, when this whole thing may well be over and done with by the end of the week, and the Duke out of harm's way."

"As you say."

"Good. I leave it to you then, Walter. Cadogan will make the necessary arrangements."

Churchill turned his head into the

pillow, closed his eyes, and was instantly asleep again.

"Marvelous, Sturmbannführer," Schellenberg said. "Allow me to congratulate you on what one can only describe as a quite brilliant achievement."

He was standing in the surgery of the doctor's clinic at the Legation watching while Kleiber lay back on the operating table, stripped to the waist.

"He's lucky," the doctor said. "Straight through the forearm and missed the bone by a hairsbreadth. You'll need a sling for at least a week, though."

He inserted three stitches very quickly, and sweat sprang to Kleiber's forehead. Sindermann stood by the door, wearing a pair of overalls the porter had found him.

"My God, and there arc those who believe we can actually win the war."

Kleiber said, between clenched teeth, "May I ask the Brigadeführer's intentions regarding the Winter girl? She may well still be with the man who came to her aid from this Bar American. If the police were to ..."

"Oh, I see, you would like me to bring the Portuguese police into this matter officially? You would prefer to bring charges, is that it,

Kleiber? It would sound nice in your daily report to the Reichsführer. How you finally cor-
nered Hannah Winter on a wharf in Lisbon with
America next stop, only you lost her again to
a man who shot you in the arm and tossed that
great ape in the corner there into the harbor."

Kleiber glared up at him, and Schellenberg
said, "No, Kleiber, I think the less the police
know about this particular incident, the better
for all concerned. I'll see you both in the morning."

He went out and found his way to Egger's
office. "Do you wish me to notify the police about
this affair, General?" Egger asked.

"No, we'll keep it to ourselves. This Joe Jackson's American Bar—do you know it?"

"Everyone knows Joe Jackson's, General, the
best night club in Lisbon. Jackson is an American who fought for the International Brigade
in Spain and flew against the Condor Legion."

"A Communist?"

"Good heavens, no. I don't think he's anything."

"Interesting. One more thing. Who is the Security Police officer with particular responsibility for the welfare of the Duke of Windsor?"

"I'm not sure. The overall commander of the
Security Police is Colonel Fernandes da Cunha."

"Is he on our side?"

Egger leaned back in his chair and considered the point. "Colonel da Cunha is a first-class policeman. One of the best I have ever known. In my opinion, I think he will follow his orders to the letter."

"Whatever those orders might be?"

"Exactly."

"Then it would appear we may well have to look a little further down the scale if we are to catch the right kind of corruption." Schellenberg glanced at his watch. "Only three o'clock. I can actually have four hours' sleep before it's time to get up."

He went out. Egger cleared his desk, then took down his coat. As he approached the door it opened and Kleiber came in. His face was very pale and his right arm was in a sling. Sindermann was behind him.

"Sturmbannführer, you should be in bed," Egger said.

"Never mind that now," Kleiber told him. "I want to know what Schellenberg was discussing with you just now."

"I can't possibly reveal that. It's a matter of confidence."

With some difficulty, Kleiber took out his wallet with his left hand and extracted Himmler's letter of authority.

"There," he said. "I act in the name of

Reichsführer Himmler himself. Perhaps you would prefer me to place a call to Berlin now to inform him of your lack of desire to co-operate in this matter?"

"No—no, of course not," said Egger, his stomach contracting at the very idea. "It was just that I hadn't fully appreciated the situation. In what way can I be of service?"

Joe Jackson ran the Mercedes in to the porch at the rear of the club, then walked back along the wharf to the stage door. As he approached, a man in a dark slouch hat and leather trench caot moved out of the shadows.

"Mr. Jackson?"

Jackson didn't need to be told who he was. He said, "Walter Schellenberg, I presume?"

"Stanley meets Livingstone, or the other way about," Schellenberg said. "Is she well?"

"She's doing all right."

Schellenberg walked to the rail and gazed into the fog. "Would it surprise you to know I wish her no harm, Mr. Jackson?"

"Why?"

"I can't explain, not even to myself. The instinct to help her has been quite unavoidable, that's all I know." He laughed without humor. "She could be the death of me yet, that girl."

"So what do you want with me?"

"There's nothing more she can achieve here. My presence, and the reason for it, has been conveyed to the British by another source entirely. Let her leave well enough alone now, for her own sake."

"And why should she believe you?"

"Why indeed?" Schellenberg lit a cigarette and for a moment the match illuminated his face. "There are occasions when I have difficulty in believing myself. Good night, Mr. Jackson."

He walked away, and even after he had faded into the fog his footsteps continued to boom hollowly on the boardwalk.

Fernandes da Cunha was small, but powerfully built with a flat, peasant face and a heavy black mustache. His father was a peasant farmer near Oporto and still alive at eighty-three. He had raised six children—five daughters and his son, Fernandes. His dearest wish was for the boy to enter the priesthood.

Fernandes had tried. Had studied hard. Had learned to speak English and Italian as well as his own language. Had given four years of his life to a Jesuit seminary outside Lisbon until a certain cold morning when he had awakened to the absolute certainty that God did not exist.

And so, he had become a policeman and in spite of, or perhaps because of, that Jesuit training, had risen steadily through every rank until he now held one of the most powerful posts of its kind in the country.

He was at his office promptly at eight o'clock that morning as was his custom. At eight-thirty he received a summons to the Presidential Palace, where he waited now for audience.

Antonio de Oliveira Salazar, President of Portugal, was fifty-one years of age. A one-time doctor of law and professor of economics, he had been virtual dictator of Portugal since 1932 and his greatest achievement had been to keep his country out of the Spanish Civil War.

He received Da Cunha alone in a small office, simply furnished, for he was a man who shunned publicity and lived a life of Spartan simplicity.

"Not for the first time, I have called you here because I have a problem of some delicacy, Colonel."

"At your orders, my President. In what way may I serve you?"

"The Duke of Windsor. A tiresome business. You may have heard that the English wish him to take up the post of Governor of the Bahamas. The Germans, on the other hand, would prefer him to stay in Europe. If they successfully invade England, they may have a use for him."

"And the problem?"

"The English seem to think it likely the Germans might try to spirit the Duke away before he leaves for the Bahamas. The German counterintelligence chief, Schellenberg, is here in person. It's all very embarrassing."

"Indeed, President."

"Especially as I've had a message from Churchill in which he says he has every confidence in our ability to see to the safety of the Duke. On the other hand, there are certain political pressures from Germany, and let's face it, it does rather look as if they're going to win."

"But if the Duke were abducted from our soil, the repercussions in America and elsewhere in the world would hardly be favorable," Da Cunha said.

"Exactly. So, what I have decided is this. If the Duke comes to a private and personal decision which takes him to Spain, well and good, but I cannot permit any act of force in the matter. I make you, Colonel da Cunha, personally responsible for his safety. You will contact the British Ambassador this morning, accompany him to the villa of Dr. Ricardo de Espirito Santo é Silva, and satisfy yourself as to the security arrangements."

"At your orders, my President." Da Cunha saluted and went out.

* * *

"You know, Sir Walford, this whole affair is really beginning to take on all the elements of a farce." The Duke of Windsor and the British Ambassador were seated together in the library. "Primo de Rivera brings me this nonsensical story from Madrid that the British Secret Service intend to take me off to the Bahamas whether I want to or not. Now you give me the same sort of yarn with the Nazis as the villains."

Sir Walford Selby tried to contain his exasperation. One of the most brilliant members of the Diplomatic Corps, he had known the Duke previously during his time as British Ambassador in Vienna in 1937.

The Lisbon posting was, by its very nature, the most crucial held by any British Ambassador outside Washington at that time, which was precisely why he had been appointed. And now, to make things even more difficult, he had the presence of the Windsors to deal with.

"I have already indicated to you my belief that your host Dr. Santo é Silva is sympathetic to the German cause, and with all due respect, sir, the presence in Lisbon of General Schellenberg should give us pause for thought."

"But good heavens, man, I'm no good to the Germans as a prisoner. Even Goebbels couldn't make much propaganda out of that situation."

"There are those who might suggest that in the context of an England under occupation, a position would be suggested to Your Royal Highness that you might feel compelled to accept, in the belief that it was in the best interests of the people."

The Duke stood up, his face dark. "That, Sir Walford, is a Judas Gate through which I would never enter."

He turned away angrily, took a cigarette from a silver box, and lit it. After a moment, he was in control again.

"Anyway, what's the time schedule?"

"There's a suitable boat leaving on the first of August, sir. For Bermuda. American. The *Excalibur*."

"Which gives us what, three days or is it four? You'll just have to see that our Secret Service people here keep a jolly good eye on me."

"At the present time, sir, the sole representative in Lisbon of the Secret Intelligence Service is Major Frear. In the situation in which our country finds itself at the moment, Portugal is of relatively little importance from an active intelligence point of view. Major Frear merely acts as a channel for double agents and paid informants."

"So what do you want me to do? Sleep with a gun under my pillow?"

There was a polite cough, and they turned to find Colonel da Cunha standing in the open French windows.

"No, sir," Sir Walford said. "The Portuguese government, being acutely aware of the dangers inherent in the situation, have assigned Colonel da Cunha to take personal charge of all arrangements for your security until the *Excalibur* leaves."

"I have inspected the grounds," Da Cunha said. "Extra men will be drafted in. I foresee no problem. Of course, it would assist if Your Royal Highness would stay within the walls."

"Now there I really can't oblige," said the Duke. "Having a day in the country tomorrow."

"May I be permitted to ask where?"

"Place called Niña. Bull farm."

Colonel da Cunha glanced at the Ambassador. "Sir, may I point out that you would be within ten miles of the Spanish border."

"The whole affair's being laid on by my good friend Primo de Rivera, the Marqués de Estella. You're surely not trying to suggest that he's going to try to run away with me!"

"No, Your Royal Highness," said Da Cunha diplomatically.

"Good. Of course, I don't mind your sending a few of your chaps along to keep us company if that will make you happy, but now, you really must excuse me. The Duchess is waiting."

He went out and Sir Walford turned to Da Cunha. "As I said, it isn't going to be easy."

As soon as he returned to his office, Da Cunha phoned Egger at the German Legation and at ten-thirty saw Schellenberg, by appointment, in a small café near the Belém Tower. He was in civilian clothes. Egger, who was with Schellenberg, made the introductions.

"General, I'll come right to the point," Da Cunha said. "Our relations with the Reich are of the friendliest at the present time, and you are a welcome guest in our country."

"But?" Schellenberg said.

"The Duke of Windsor is a special case. We desire nothing more than to see him board ship on the first of August and sail away to Bermuda. Until then, President Salazar has made me personally responsible for his welfare. I have increased the guards at the villa and they have orders to shoot any intruder. Do I make myself clear?"

"As crystal," Schellenberg said. "And now, my dear Colonel, a cognac to sweeten your coffee."

"My pleasure," Fernandes da Cunha told him.

* * *

Joe Jackson telephoned Frear at his apartment just after ten. It was some time before he got an answer, and Frear sounded annoyed, as if he'd just been awakened from a sound sleep.

"It's Jackson. What's happening?"

"What do you mean, what's happening?"

"About what we discussed last night!"

"Nothing new in that, old boy. Thought I made that clear. I've reported it to my people, of course. I'm sure they'll take appropriate action."

"If they're anything like you, they couldn't find their way to the men's room," Jackson said.

"Now look here, Joseph," Frear told him angrily. "This is none of your affair, so stay out of it. If you want my advice, that girl friend of yours had better keep her head down as well or she might get it knocked off."

He put down the receiver. Jackson sat there, thinking about it for a while, then dressed and left quickly. It was raining when he went downstairs and got into the Mercedes. He turned into the main road and started along the waterfront.

Behind him, a Buick pulled out from behind a large produce truck. Schellenberg said to Zeidler, the driver whom the Legation had provided, "Take your time, stay well back. If you lose him, I'll have your balls."

He leaned back in the seat and lit a cigarette.

* * *

There was no sign of Hannah in the house at Cascais. Jackson left the car in the courtyard and walked back down the track to the beach. The Buick had pulled into the pine trees a good hundred yards away, and Schellenberg watched through field glasses.

It was a fine, warm day, and down below the village the beach was stacked with fishing boats painted in vivid hues of every description.

Fishermen sat mending their nets, children playing around them, and beyond, the long Atlantic combers rolled in.

Jackson saw her walking toward him barefoot, carrying a bucket, men, young and old, looking up at her in frank admiration as she passed. She saw him and started to run.

"What a marvelous day," she said. "And this place. The people are wonderful. So friendly and courteous, and the boats." She turned to look at them. "Why do some of them have eyes painted on the prows?"

"That's debatable," he said. "Some say to ward off the evil one. Others, so the ship can find its way through any storm. I see you've been buying fish."

"Yes, have you eaten?"

"No."

"Then you're in luck. As my mother raised me to be a nice Jewish girl that means I'm a wonderful cook." She took his arm and as they walked back toward the house said, "You told me you'd see the right people—did you?"

"Yes, and when I got back to the club your friend Schellenberg was waiting to see me."

"My friend? Why do you say that?"

"Because in a strange kind of way, I think he is."

"What did he want?"

"He said the British knew why he was here so there was no reason for you to continue to get involved. That he wanted you to stay out of it."

She was troubled now, he could see it on her face, and they walked the rest of the way in silence.

And she was indeed a good cook. The fish was delicious, but she didn't do more than pick at it herself and stared down into her coffee, her face moody.

"All right, what is it?" he asked.

"It just doesn't seem right. I don't get the feeling that anyone's taking the thing seriously enough." She leaned across the table. "It's no good, Joe. I want to see him myself. Tell him to his face. What he does then is his affair, but unless I do it that way, I'll always feel that somehow I let Uncle Max down."

"Okay." He sighed. "There's someone I can try. A man I know called Taniguchi who can fix most things. I'll go and see what he can do, but it could cost money."

"I've got an American Express credit letter for two thousand dollars."

"For that he'd probably kidnap the Duke himself. I'll see what he says."

"Now?" she said.

"You mean right this minute?" He shook his head in mock resignation. "Women. My old granny always warned me against them. Okay. I'll take a run into town. You keep your head down. I'll be back when I can, but it could take most of the day."

She watched him drive away and, on impulse, went down the track, kicked off her shoes, and walked on the beach again. The sun was very warm now. She flung herself down in the sand next to a fishing boat and closed her eyes.

She heard footsteps approach. A familiar voice said, "Hello, Hannah."

When she opened her eyes, Walter Schellenberg was standing beside her.

"I must say you're really looking very well indeed, all things considered."

She said, "What do you want with me?"

"Cigarette?" He offered her one, and she took

it without thinking. When he gave her a light, there was a curious intimacy to the gesture. She drew back as if to put distance between them.

"I asked you what you wanted."

"Nothing," he said. "Or rather, I wish you to do nothing from now on. You can no longer alter the course of events, Hannah. The game is in progress, and the players on both sides know the score—isn't that your American phrase?"

"Is that how you see it? Just a game?"

"Of course it is—a great and terrible game that, once started, is impossible to stop. The game controls us, Hannah, we don't control the game. It's like a fairground carousel. Once it's in motion, that's it."

"You could always try jumping off."

"Too late for that now. I'm trapped along with thousands like me. You think I believe that madman back there in Berlin? Do you honestly think that I believe in even one word of his lies? Blacks are inferior, which means I can't enjoy the music of your Connie Jones. The Führer in his wisdom had decreed that Einstein can't count up to ten, and the fact that Hannah Winter has a voice to . . ."

"I don't want to hear any more of this." She got to her feet, her hands to her ears for a moment.

"You got me out of Prinz Albrechtstrasse, God knows why, but you did, and you helped Connie and the boys in Madrid, but you killed Uncle Max. It doesn't matter whose finger was on the trigger. You killed Uncle Max."

They stood there, confronting each other. There was only the sound of the sea on the shore, a gull's cry. And then it was as if something broke inside her.

"Why?" she whispered and there was pain in her voice. "I don't understand."

He put a hand under her chin and smiled gently. "Life, my Hannah, has a habit on occasion of seizing one by the throat and refusing to let go. It's really very sad."

He kissed her gently on the mouth, turned, and walked away. For a long time after he had gone, she simply sat there, staring out to sea, then she got up and walked slowly back to the house.

TWELVE

UNLIKE THE previous evening, the warehouse was a hive of industry when Schellenberg entered and went up the iron staircase to Taniguchi's office. The big Japanese was dictating letters to a young secretary, but he sent her out, shutting the door.

"Anything for me?" Schellenberg asked.

"But of course."

Taniguchi opened a cupboard to disclose a wall safe which he unlocked. He took out a manila folder. "Everything you need, Walter. A plan of the villa and the grounds. A list of the servants. They are provided by an agency in town in which I have a business interest. I have already arranged that as from this morning, an under-footman, a maid, and an assistant gardener will be replaced by people in my pay. They all speak reasonable English."

"Excellent—and the police?"

"Slightly more difficult. Colonel da Cunha, head of Security Police, has been placed in charge of security at the villa personally. The rumor is that his orders come from Salazar himself."

"I've already heard he is a first-rate policeman, that one."

"Certainly beyond any bribe," Taniguchi said. "Luckily, the officer who is actually stationed at the villa for the duration of the Duke's stay is a different specimen entirely. One Captain José Mota."

"Is he on our side?"

"If you're referring to ideologies, no, but he does have appallingly expensive tastes, particularly in women. So, what are your orders?"

"For the moment, what I require is general information about what's going on in the house itself. Any conversation these people of yours can overhear would be useful."

"About the Duke's future plans? And what if he decides to go to the Bahamas after all, Walter? What then?"

"I wouldn't blame him really." Schellenberg got up. "I hear the climate's delightful."

Taniguchi laughed uproariously. "It really is most amusing."

"What is?"

"Life, or its more ridiculous aspects. Now take something as abstract as information, Walter. A commodity as subject to the forces of the market place as any other. Something which may, for example, be sold not only once, but twice."

"An interesting hypothesis," Schellenberg said. "Let's discuss it." He sat down again.

Huene was having his morning coffee when Schellenberg was shown into his office.

"Ah, there you are, General. Care to join me?"

"That would be nice."

Huene poured coffee into another cup and pushed a message across. "There's something for you from the Foreign Office which you may not appreciate quite as much. I've had it decoded."

It was from Ribbentrop and very much to the point.

> At a suitable occasion, the Duke must be informed that Germany wants peace with the English people, that the Churchill clique stands in the way of it, and that it would be a good thing if the Duke would hold himself in

readiness for further developments. Germany is determined to force England to peace by every means of power and upon this happening would be prepared to accommodate any desire expressed by the Duke, especially with a view to the assumption of the English throne by the Duke and Duchess...

There was more in the same vein, including the fact that Ribbentrop believed Espirito Santo é Silva to be sympathetic to German aims. There was also a reiteration of the rumor that the British Secret Service had designs on the Duke's person.

"Well, that's certainly explicit enough," Schellenberg said.

"I've heard from Primo de Rivera," Huene told him. "He's taking the Windsors out for the day tomorrow to visit a bull farm. Rather interesting, the one he has chosen. It's at a place called Niña. Only ten miles from the Spanish border. I've had my confidential secretary type up a report of the conversation he had with me. There's your copy."

Schellenberg read it quickly. "I see he intends to pursue the matter of this so-called British plot."

"You find it nonsense?"

"Frankly, yes."

"Would it be in any way absurd to suggest that if anything unfortunate happened to him, it could always be blamed on us?"

"Nothing, I find, is impossible in this wicked old world of ours. I see he suggests that the Duke's host is sympathetic to our view of things. I suppose that could be considered useful."

"So, what do you intend to do?"

"Wait to see the outcome of De Rivera's day out in the country with the Windsors. If he persuades the Duke that to flee to Spain would be in his best interest—if the Duke actually wants to be persuaded—then the border, from what you tell me, is only twenty minutes' fast drive from Niña. Ribbentrop and the Führer will be delighted and we can all go home."

"And if the Duke decides otherwise?"

Schellenberg smiled and stood up. "The coffee, Baron, was really quite excellent. I'll see you later."

The American Bar was a popular rendezvous at lunchtime and it was crowded when Kajiro Taniguchi entered just after two o'clock. Joe Jackson was seated on a stool at the far end of the bar talking to a couple of customers. He left them and came across at once.

"You getting anywhere?"

"I think you could say that."

Jackson led the way upstairs to his office and closed the door. "All right—what's the deal?"

"A busy man, this Duke of yours. Tomorrow, he goes with Primo de Rivera to visit the bull farm of Antonio de Oliveira outside Niña."

Jackson frowned. "That's getting awfully close to the Spanish border."

"Yes, isn't it? However, to stick with the villa. Although Fernandes da Cunha has overall responsibility for the Duke, the officer in charge at the villa at all times is one Captain José Mota."

"And he's bribable?"

"Corrupt as a week-old corpse, but it's going to cost you, Joe. One thousand dollars in American money—nothing less. And he wants it in advance."

"What do we get for that?"

"Every night at ten o'clock, the Duke has a final cigar while taking a walk in the garden. Always goes alone. I've got a small plan."

He took a square of paper from his wallet and unfolded it. "Down here, below the swimming pool in this corner, there's a summerhouse. The Duke always ends his walk sitting in there for five minutes finishing his cigar."

"So?"

"Just a few yards away from it in this area?" He pointed. "It's a shrubbery concealing a door in the wall. Usually, there's a policeman discreetly on guard, but tonight, if you're interested, there won't be. What's more, it will be unlocked."

"Thanks to Captain Mota?"

"Exactly."

"Who expects his cash in advance?"

"I'm afraid so."

Jackson went to the large old-fashioned safe in the corner, unlocked it, brought a cash box to the desk, and counted out ten one-hundred-dollar bills.

"One more thing," Taniguchi said. "The young lady goes in alone."

"Now look here," Jackson began.

"Part of the deal, Joe. Either you agree, or it's all off. She leaves the car halfway down the hill and walks the rest of the way. That's so the gate sentry doesn't hear her."

Jackson shrugged. "Okay," he said reluctantly. "But I expect service for this little lot, old buddy, and if I don't get it..."

"Trust, Joe, another of this world's more salable commodities. You must learn to value it."

Taniguchi was smiling as he went out of the door.

* * *

Huene placed an office at Schellenberg's disposal, small but perfectly adequate. He was working at the desk when there was a knock at the door and Kleiber entered. He was still very pale and now carried his right arm in a sling made from a silk scarf.

"Well, what do you want?" Schellenberg asked.

"I assumed there would be work to do."

"As I understood it, your task was to act as my bodyguard," Schellenberg told him. "You're obviously totally unfit for that at the moment, so my orders are that you go to bed until fully recovered."

"And Sindermann?"

"Is of no use to me whatsoever."

"But the Duke of Windsor, General?"

"Is none of your affair, so do as I order. Do you understand?"

"Jawohl, Brigadeführer," Kleiber said, but when he turned to the door there was murder in his eyes.

Five minutes later he entered Egger's office without ceremony, Sindermann at his heels.

"Sturmbannführer?" Egger said in alarm.

Kleiber sat down. "In the matter of General Schellenberg, my worst fears have been realized. There can be little doubt that he is not pursuing his orders as regards this Windsor affair with anything like the vigor he should. Have you anything to report to me?"

Egger looked hunted, but replied in a low voice, "Yes, I think so. No more than an hour ago he received a brief visit from Captain José Mota of the Security Police, the officer in charge of the detachment at the villa."

"Here?" Kleiber said. "He actually came here?"

"Nothing unusual in that, Sturmbannführer. He often calls here to see me to discuss matters where police cooperation is required."

"You know him socially?"

"Yes, Sturmbannführer."

"I see. Have you any idea of the substance of his talk with General Schellenberg?"

"No."

"But you could find out from your friend Mota, I'm sure?"

"I could try, Sturmbannführer."

"Then do so, by all means," Kleiber told him. "And as soon as possible."

It was just before ten when Hannah turned into the hill road leading up to the villa. Following Taniguchi's instructions, she pulled into the grass shoulder under the trees halfway up the hill, parked, and started to walk the rest of the way.

A couple of minutes later, there was the softest of clicks as the passenger door opened and Joe Jackson, who had been crouched on the floor, slid out. He wore black pants and sweater, a balaclava helmet pulled over his face so that only his eyes showed. The Browning was tucked into his belt at the rear.

He went after her, keeping to the trees. The gate in the wall was clearly visible because there was a small light above it. He saw her pause, then tentatively try the handle. The door opened to her touch. She passed inside.

Some distance further along there was a tree conveniently close to the wall, its branches spreading across. Jackson climbed up quickly, poised on top of the wall to slide over, then saw the dim bulk of the summerhouse only four or five yards away. There was a lantern on the inside of the door also, and in its light, he could see Hannah approaching. He reached for the Browning at his back and held it ready. The girl hesitated and stepped up on to the veranda.

She could see the glow in the darkness, smell the aroma of good Havana. "Your Royal Highness," she whispered. "Please—I must speak with you. My name is..."

"Hannah Winter," Walter Schellenberg said.

He moved out of the shadows and stood on the porch. "Oh, my God," she said and turned to run, only to find her way blocked by a young police officer.

Schellenberg said, "It's all right, Mota, I'll return the young lady to her car now. Better lock the door after us."

He had a hand on her elbow, taking her back down the path to the door. They went out, and Mota closed it behind them.

Flat on the wall, Jackson heard Schellenberg say to the girl, "I'm afraid Taniguchi wasn't exactly honest with your friend, Mr. Jackson. The Duke doesn't turn up for another half hour yet. What am I going to do with you, Hannah? Didn't I tell you to stay out of this thing?"

Jackson would have slipped off the wall to follow then, but Mota had paused only a few yards away to light a cigarette. The match flared, illuminating a handsome, rather weak face.

He peered around furtively, then whispered in Portuguese, "All right, you can come out now."

Kleiber and Sindermann emerged from the bushes.

"You saw what you wanted?" Mota asked.

"Oh, yes," Kleiber answered in Portuguese.

"The General is certainly going to have some explaining to do when we return to Berlin. However, let us discuss tomorrow's events. When do you leave for this bull farm?"

"Nine-thirty. The Duke and Duchess with the Marqués de Estella and their driver in the Buick. Two police motorcyclists lead the way one mile in advance. I follow with half a dozen men in a police truck; the Buick is last in line."

"So?"

"Three miles before you reach Niña there is a village called Rosario. An inn and a few houses—nothing more. They don't even have a telephone. I'll arrange for the truck to break down. No problem there—the driver is very much my man. When the Buick reaches us, I'll tell them to carry on and wait for us at Rosario."

"Where the motorcyclists will already have passed through?"

"Exactly. Eleven, give or take a few minutes, is the time I estimate the Buick should arrive and if you and your man here are waiting." He shrugged. "A simple matter to take over at pistol point and drive to the border. Twenty minutes and you'll be in Spain."

"Excellent," Kleiber said. "You've done well."

"And General Schellenberg?"

"Is to know nothing."

"So what about my money?"

"You'll get it, you have my word on that. Twenty thousand American dollars, just as we agreed."

Jackson didn't wait to hear any more, but allowed himself to slide gently over the wall and dropped into the damp grass. He started back down the hill where Hannah had left the Mercedes, but it had gone.

The contingency plan had been simple: if they lost touch, to try and rendezvous at the beach house at Cascais, which was almost two miles away. As he started to trot along the grass verge at the side of the road, it began to rain.

When Hannah and Schellenberg reached the Mercedes, he held open the door for her, then went around to the other side and got into the passenger seat.

"I came by cab myself. You don't mind giving me a lift back into Lisbon, do you?"

She started the car and drove away, thinking of Joe Jackson back there at the villa. "As far as the first cab rank."

He lit two cigarettes and passed one over to her. "You must see now what nonsense it is for you to continue to interfere in this business. The fact that you found me waiting for you in the summerhouse tonight, instead of the Duke,

must surely prove to you that I have more influence in Lisbon than even your Mr. Jackson."

As they neared the Tower of Belém they came
to a night club with a neon sign flashing on and
off in the dark. A couple of cabs were drawn up
in front and she pulled in at the curb.

She didn't say a word and Schellenberg got
out, closed the door, then leaned in at the window and smiled. "We really can't go on meeting
this way, you realize that, don't you?"

She swung the Mercedes around in a U-turn
and drove away rapidly.

Lights were on in the house when she stopped
in the courtyard. As she went up the steps to
the veranda, the door opened and Jackson appeared. He was stripped to the waist and toweling himself down.

"What happened?"

She told him.

"You missed the best part of the show," he
said, as she followed him inside. "After you'd
gone, your two friends from the wharf turned
up—Kleiber and Sindermann. Seems they don't
exactly see eye to eye with Schellenberg. They've
cooked up a plot with Captain Mota to snatch
the Duke and Duchess on the way to the bull
farm at Niña tomorrow. That young man is cer-

tainly in the market for corruption. Seems to be holding his hand out to everyone."

"Can we stop it?"

"Oh, yes, I think so. I've already found out who is putting on the show in the ring at Niña tomorrow. I rang the union."

"The union?"

"Sure—bullfighters have a union, just like anyone else. You know, I'm beginning to think this whole business this evening could turn out to be to our advantage."

"How?"

"Never mind that now. I'll explain on the way into town. Make me some coffee while I change."

When he reappeared five minutes later he was wearing black tie and white tuxedo. "Working clothes," he told her. "After all, I *am* a saloonkeeper."

She handed him his coffee. "I've been thinking. The friend of yours who laid things on for us at the villa didn't exactly come up with value for money."

"Oh, I don't know," Jackson said. "The Nazis have not only been printing their own money lately, but other people's as well. Their British five-pound notes are excellent and their American one-hundred-dollar bills aren't bad. As long as you don't look at them too closely, that is. Someone tried to pass a few off at my gaming tables the other month. I confiscated them, naturally, and tossed him out on his ear. Not worth bothering the police, and it did seem a use might turn up for them some time."

"You bastard," she said in awe.

"I like to think so."

The café they stopped at was on the edge of the Alfama district and fronting on the river. It had no name. She could hear singing and guitar music.

"Shouldn't I be asking myself what a young girl like me is doing in a place like this?"

"This is no ordinary bar," he said. "More like a club."

When they went in, she saw at once what he meant. The walls were covered with posters advertising various bullfights, and several bulls' heads were mounted behind the bar.

It was not particularly busy. A young man leaned against the wall, chair tilted, playing a guitar and singing a *fado* softly. Four men played cards at another table. One of them was a small, dark, fierce-looking man with a dreadful scar on one cheek running into the eye.

He called cheerfully, "Olá, Senhor Joe! Five minutes only. I have the hand of a lifetime here."

"I told you I phoned the union," Jackson said.

"And this is it. That's José Borges, local union president. He used to be one of the greatest *toureiros* in the game until he took a horn in the face and lost an eye. Lot of gypsy blood in him."

The barkeeper brought coffee in heavy glasses and brandy, without being told, and went away again. There was a cry of joy at the card table, general laughter, and José Borges got up and crossed to join them.

There was a patch over his right eye, she saw that now as Jackson said, "Senhorita Winter— José Borges. Little José to every lover of the bulls in Portugal, for twenty-two years now."

"Senhorita." He took her hand and bowed gravely.

Jackson said, "I hear Oliveira has hired you to put on the show at his farm at Niña tomorrow for the Duke of Windsor and the Marqués de Estella. A proud day for you."

"There have been others," Borges said modestly and lit a long black cheroot.

"I was wondering whether we can join you? Senhorita Winter, who is an American like myself, has never seen a bullfight. That being so, it seems to me she should see the best, and as you fight so seldom these days, José, tomorrow would really be a unique opportunity."

Borges turned with interest to Hannah. "So, you have a love for the bulls, senhorita?"

"I'm not sure," she said. "I'll have to see. It's the killing part of it that worries me."

He roared with laughter. "This is Portugal, not Spain. Here, the only one to get killed is the *toureiro* if he is unlucky. Once, many years ago, the Count of Arcos was torn to pieces by a bull before the eyes of the whole court. The Queen declared that Portugal was too weak to risk the life of a man against that of a bull. Since that day, the putting of the bull to death has been prohibited."

"The tips of the horns are covered with leather," Jackson said. "Leather sheaths. But often, in the middle of a fight, they come off."

"And then, senhorita," said Borges, running a finger along his scar. "You're in trouble."

"So, you'll take us tomorrow?" Jackson asked.

"All right. We leave at eight."

"We'll come with you in the truck, if that's all right."

"Fine."

"Good." Jackson got up. "We'd better get moving. I've got a club to run."

The sign *Joe Jackson's American Bar* was bright in the night and there were a great many cars parked outside. He left the Mercedes on the wharf and took her in the side entrance and up the back stairs to his office.

When he slid back a panel in the wall, it revealed a black grill through which they could look down into the gaming room. Dice, blackjack, poker—they were all doing well, but the crowd around the roulette wheel was particularly heavy.

Jackson said, "Good, there he is. You wait here."

Colonel Fernandes da Cunha was not doing particularly well. Jackson said, "Hello, Fernandes. I always thought twelve was your lucky number."

"Did you, Joe?" Da Cunha smiled. "Then twelve it is, by all means."

As the wheel stopped, the ball slotted neatly into place. Jackson said, "I'd let it ride, if I were you."

"Who am I to argue with the proprietor."

This time, when twelve came up again, he picked up the chips the croupier pushed toward him. "You're being excessively generous tonight, Joe, I wonder why."

"Oh, I haven't even started yet," Jackson told him. "Come upstairs and have a drink. You might find it interesting."

Hannah was standing at the grill looking

down into the gaming room as they entered. She turned and Jackson said. "Fernandes, I'd like to introduce Miss Hannah Winter. Now, you could arrest her. On the other hand, if you're as smart as I think you are, you'll listen to what we've got to say first."

THIRTEEN

IT WAS A fine bright morning as the old truck rolled along the dusty road between the olive trees, women in black dresses and straw hats already at work in the fields.

Hannah and Jackson were up front in the cab beside Borges, who was driving himself. The other members of his team were in the rear.

Hannah was in a peasant dress and headscarf which Jackson had procured for her. He wore a tweed cap, a collarless shirt and an old jacket many times patched. It interested her that Borges had made no comment on their appearance.

At one point, he fished out a packet of cheap

local cigarettes with one hand. She got one out
for him, lit it and put it into his mouth.

"My thanks."

"You and Joe—you've known each other
long?"

"Since Spain, senhorita. We fought together
against Franco. Starved together. It was a bad
time, I can tell you. A few drops of olive oil in
water, a handful of grapes. Sometimes we didn't
see a loaf of bread for weeks."

Jackson was dozing in the corner. She looked
at him and said, "Hardly worth the money, I
should have thought."

"Money?" he laughed hoarsely. "For the last
year of the war we didn't get a peso—not any
of us."

Hannah glanced again at Jackson, perplexed.
"But I thought..."

"That we fought for money, Joe and I? But
you are wrong."

"Then why did you fight?"

"I ask him that question myself once. For me,
it's simple. I'm a Communist, but Joe just said
he didn't like Franco." At that moment, they
rumbled past a small inn with tables outside
and half a dozen houses. "Ah, Rosario. We'll
soon be there."

"You know something?" Joe Jackson said,
without opening his eyes. "You talk too much."

* * *

In the rear of the Buick, Primo de Rivera was seated opposite the Duke and Duchess.

The Duke said, "It really is too much. Wallis received a bunch of flowers this morning. Anonymous, mind you. The card said: *Beware of the machinations of the British Secret Service. A Portuguese friend who has your interests at heart.* Have you ever heard such rot?"

"Such talk is common in Madrid," De Rivera said.

"Good God, Primo, it's absolutely bloody nonsense. I mean, there is no British Secret Service in Lisbon at the moment. Well, hardly anything worth speaking about. I know, believe me."

The Buick slowed as they came alongside the police truck parked at the side of the road. Captain Mota approached and saluted. "I regret the inconvenience, Your Royal Highness. A minor breakdown and soon rectified. If you would continue to Rosario and wait for us there."

"Very well," said the Duke and nodded to the chauffeur. "Drive on."

Kleiber and Sindermann arrived at the inn at Rosario at ten-thirty in a rented car from Lisbon. Kleiber paid the driver off and they went inside. It was a poor place—rough-cast

walls, stone floor, and wooden tables—and
there were no other customers.

An old woman appeared from a room at the
rear to serve them. They ordered red wine and
a plate of olives for something to do and sat at
a table by the window.

Kleiber glanced at his watch. "Check your
gun."

They had both obtained Walthers from the
armory at the Legation. The Sturmbannführer
handled his with conscious pleasure as he
pulled the slider, putting a round into the
breech, and slipped on the safety catch with
difficulty because of his sling.

The two police motorcyclists roared by, rais-
ing dust outside. "Not long now. I'd like to see
Schellenberg's face when he hears about this."

"Why wait?" Schellenberg said, walking in
from the kitchen followed by Da Cunha and a
couple of policemen with machine pistols.

"I see you've beaten us to it, gentlemen," Da
Cunha said. "We, too, are here to see the Duke
drive past."

"Colonel da Cunha is head of the Security
Police," Schellenberg explained. "He's just had
the distressing task of arresting one of his own
officers."

"An unfortunate case," Da Cunha said. "A
most corrupt young man."

At that moment, the Buick appeared and slowed to a halt. Da Cunha straightened his tunic and went out. They saw him salute, then lean down at the window. He drew back and the Buick continued.

He returned. "Right, I'll follow them to Niña personally, just to make certain the rest of the day passes uneventfully. You are returning to Lisbon now, I presume, General?"

"Yes, I think so," Schellenberg said. "My thanks, Colonel."

He went out through the kitchen, and Kleiber and Sindermann followed. The Embassy Buick was waiting in the yard, Zeidler standing beside it.

"We could have had him, damn you!" Kleiber said. "Don't you realize that?"

"Interesting," Schellenberg remarked. "The Duke and I having the same car, I mean. It proves something, though I'm not sure what."

Bullfighting in Portugal when performed in gala dress is a spectacular sight. The De Oliveira ranch boasted its own ring and for the royal party mounted a dazzling performance.

The first two bulls were fought from horseback in approved style, their host himself, as is common with many Portuguese noblemen, taking part dressed in cloth of gold with satin breeches and a tricorn hat with ostrich plumes.

But the Duke and Duchess soon found the display, in spite of the incredible skill with which the horses were ridden, a bore.

The spectacle which followed, *las pegas*, was much more interesting. The *torril* was opened and a bull launched himself like a black thunderbolt into the sunlight. He stood there, pawing the ground. A line of men, in traditional costume, moved into the arena, headed by José Borges.

The Duke said, "What do they intend to do?"

Primo de Rivera said, "It's rather fascinating. Your Royal Highness has visited Greece, of course. On Cretan vases you will see depicted the dances of the sacred bull in which young men did handsprings on the bulls' horns."

"Are you trying to tell me these chaps are going to do something similar?"

The line of men advanced to meet the bull. José Borges challenged the beast, supremely arrogant, head thrown back, hands on hips, offering himself as a target.

As the bull charged, the Duchess cried out in alarm, but at the last moment, Borges flung himself on the animal's head, grabbed its horns, and did a handspring, leaping from its back as it thundered on. He turned, hands on hips again, and bowed to the royal party, who applauded.

Two of his companions repeated the trick and finally Borges performed again, standing on the bull's back after his somersault this time, and staying there for a full minute while it cantered around the ring. When he jumped down, the gates of the *torril* were reopened and the oxen driven in to fetch the bull.

"What happens to him now?" the Duchess asked their host, De Oliveira, who had joined them again.

"Sometimes he is slaughtered, or if he is brave, he is returned to the pastures and kept for breeding. A bull may never be put into the arena twice. Once he has learned the ropes, so to speak, he would be too dangerous."

"So I can imagine."

"If I might present some of the *toureiros* to Your Royal Highness now. A moment only. It would be a great honor for them."

"Most certainly," the Duke said. "I'd particularly like to meet the chappie with the eye patch. Remarkable performance. Quite astonishing."

Luncheon was served on the wide terrace at the rear of the ranch house under the spreading branches of a eucalyptus tree, its perfume scent-

ing the air. De Oliveira had deliberately kept
the meal traditional. Cold *gaspacho,* a soup of
bread soaked in water and vinegar with chopped
raw vegetables, salty smoked sausages, crisp
salads, and fresh ewe cheese.

The one sophisticated concession to the occasion was the plentiful supply of champagne:
Dom Perignon in silver buckets of ice heavily
emblazoned with the De Oliveira coat of arms.

The Duke smiled lazily at the Duchess. "Enjoyed it, Wallis?"

"Oh, yes, David, the most wonderful day
we've had in ages."

"Just thinking that myself. Still, time to be
getting back now."

Primo de Rivera seemed about to say something, but at that moment Fernandes da Cunha
approached across the lawn.

"Ready for the off, Colonel, I think," the Duke
said.

Da Cunha saluted. "If Your Royal Highness
would be so kind as to spare me a few minutes
in private. A question of security."

"Certainly." The Duke smiled at the others.
"Do excuse me. Shan't be long, I'm sure."

He walked across the lawn smoking a cigarette, Da Cunha keeping pace with him. "Now
look here, Colonel," he said. "I don't know what
sort of wild rumors you've heard, but when I

leave here ten minutes from now, my car will be pointing in the general direction of Lisbon. I have no intention, no matter what some people seem to think, of making a dash for the Spanish border."

"Earlier today, Your Royal Highness avoided, by a hairsbreadth, a situation that would have given you no choice in the matter."

They were crossing the courtyard and had reached the small stone chapel which served the estate.

The Duke paused and said, "Good God, Colonel, what on earth are you talking about?"

Colonel da Cunha opened the chapel door and removed his cap. "If Your Royal Highness would care to step inside, there is someone waiting who will be able to explain the situation far better than I ever could."

It was a tiny, simple chapel with a stone floor and whitewashed walls. There was a statue of the Virgin at one side, candles flickering before it, the plainest of altars, with a carved wooden crucifix.

Two peasants, a man and a woman, were sitting on one of the rough wooden benches toward the front of the chapel. At the sound of the door opening, they turned and stood up and the Duke saw that the woman was young and rather pretty, in black peasant dress and scarf. When she started to speak and it became apparent that she was American, he was quite astonished.

Afterward, they sat there on the bench, the three of them together, Da Cunha standing close at hand.

"It really is the most extraordinary business I ever heard of in my life," the Duke said.

"But true, sir, every word," Hannah told him.

"Oh, I believe you, my dear, never fear. Colonel da Cunha's account of the near miss at Rosario this morning confirms it." He turned to Da Cunha. "You say General Schellenberg told you there was no question of abduction in his mind?"

"Yes, sir, he assured me that as far as he was concerned, the choice of what action to take in this affair was entirely up to Your Royal Highness."

"And you believe him?"

"Yes, sir, I do. There can be no doubt whatever that Sturmbannführer Kleiber and his man were acting on their own initiative in the matter. As Senhorita Winter's story has indicated, General Schellenberg is a rather unusual man in many respects."

"Indeed he is." The Duke sat there, frowning,

then looked up at Da Cunha intently. "Colonel—can I rely on your good offices?"

"Sir, President Salazar has made me personally responsible for your safety while you are on the soil of Portugal, with my life, if necessary."

"I can trust you? Your word on it as an officer and a gentleman?"

"As a man, sir. My father was a peasant farmer from Oporto."

The Duke smiled faintly. "Yes, of course. And General Schellenberg and his friends?"

"Delicate, sir. There is a political understanding between my country and Germany at the moment which puts us in a most unusual situation. The Germans are the masters of Europe, and if we were to expel General Schellenberg and Kleiber and this other fellow . . ."

"No—that wouldn't be the right way to tackle it at all." The Duke turned to Joe Jackson. "And you, Mr. Jackson? We often speak of the special relationship between our two countries. In my own case, more true than it is of most Englishmen. May I also rely on you?"

"Of course, sir."

"Good." The Duke turned to Hannah and took her hands. "As for you, my dear, how can I ask for more when you have done so very much already?"

She was almost crying, fought to control the tears, and his hands tightened on hers for a moment. Then he released her.

"May I inquire as to Your Royal Highness' plans?" Da Cunha asked.

"Easily answered, Colonel. I intend to leave on the *Excalibur* the day after tomorrow. In spite of all the speculation, I shall take up my appointment in the Bahamas as requested by Mr. Churchill."

"And in the meantime?"

"Back to Estoril. May I ask, Colonel, if you will be at the villa later in the day?"

"I shall make the lodge at the main gate my headquarters," Fernandes da Cunha told him. "From where I shall be available to Your Royal Highness at any time of the night or day."

"Excellent." The Duke was frowning slightly. "I may need you later on. There's something stirring at the back of my mind. I'm not sure what yet, but it will surface. It usually does. And now, I think, I'd really better be getting back to the others."

Later that day at a special meeting held in the Chancellery for only the most important members of his government, Hitler announced that he was issuing Directive Number 17, the official order for Goering to make preparations for the air attack on England that was to be the preliminary to invasion. He then outlined, in finest detail, Sea Lion, the plan of campaign that would culminate in his own triumphal drive into London.

Afterward, as they were all leaving, he ordered Ribbentrop to remain. The Reichsminister was closeted with him for a most uncomfortable five minutes. When he finally left, he found Himmler waiting.

"You don't look too happy, Reichsminister."

"The Windsor affair," Ribbentrop said. "The Duke is more essential to our plans than ever now that Sea Lion has been finalized."

"But will he see things our way?"

"The Führer is no longer interested in whether he will or not. He has given me instructions to order the Duke's immediate abduction."

"Then you'd better get in touch with Schellenberg as soon as possible, hadn't you?" Himmler said.

Ribbentrop was angry and a little frightened. "Damn the man. I haven't heard from him once since he's been in Portugal. Not once."

He walked away quickly. Himmler watched him go, his face calm, then he left himself, went down the steps of the Reich Chancellery to his car, and was driven back to Prinz Albrechtstrasse.

* * *

At the Legation, Schellenberg was standing at the window of his office drinking coffee when the door opened abruptly and Kleiber entered. His face was contorted with anger and he was waving a message in one hand.

"You received this an hour ago."

Schellenberg took the message from him and read it quickly. It was a copy of Ribbentrop's signal.

"My goodness, Kleiber, you certainly must have influence. I congratulate you. This was supposed to be confidential and for my eyes only."

"It's a direct order from the Führer to abduct the Duke of Windsor. Now, what are you going to do about it?"

"I'll let you know, if and when I think it necessary. On the way out, I'd prefer you to close the door behind you without slamming it."

Kleiber returned to the anteroom where Sindermann waited. "Nothing!" he raged. "Nothing, Gunter!"

He made his decision, turned, and hurried along to the communications room. He asked the duty officer for a signal pad and wrote on it with difficulty because of his right arm still in the sling:

General Schellenberg shows no serious intention of completing mission as
instructed. Please confirm with the
Ambassador my powers to take over
in this matter.

Signed Kleiber

He handed it to the duty officer. "Encode that
now. Priority One. Most immediate and for the
eyes of the Reichsführer Himmler only."

Himmler was writing away at his desk when
one of his aides entered. "Signal from Lisbon,
Reichsführer. Sturmbannführer Kleiber."

Himmler read it then said, "Send a reply at
once, not to Kleiber, but to Ambassador Huene."

He started to dictate in dry precise tones, his
voice like leaves rustling in a wood at evening.

As dusk was falling that same evening the
Duchess went into the garden in search of the
Duke. She found him sitting on the edge of the
fountain, smoking his pipe, gazing into the
water pensively.

"There you are," she said. "I've been looking
everywhere. There's a letter for you from Sir

Walford. The messenger didn't stay. He said his instructions were that no answer was required."

"Thank you, my dear." He opened it and read the contents quickly. He smiled as he passed it across to her. "Walter Monckton's due in by plane some time tomorrow."

"How nice," she said, "to see Walter again, but why?"

"Oh, Winston making sure nothing goes wrong at the last moment. Walter, after all, has always been the Government's general purpose man where I am concerned. You are right, though. It will be nice to see him again. A friendly face to wave good-bye from the dock as we sail away into oblivion because, God help me, Wallis, that's the only way I can see it."

"Saint Helena, nineteen-forty," she said. "Now I know how Napoleon must have felt."

"I wanted to do something in this war, something useful, but they won't let me, you see?" He laughed softly. "Rather ironic, when you come to think of it, but the only people who do seem to want me are the Nazis."

And suddenly, he was no longer smiling, his face tense and excited. "My God, I wonder?"

"Wonder what, David? What are you talking about?"

"How far they'd be willing to go. If they want me badly enough, that is."

"David." There was total shock in her voice. "You couldn't."

"No, you don't understand, my dear. What I'm talking about is a possibility, a faint one only perhaps, that I might be able to extract something of value from this situation. Not to me, you understand, but to Britain." He seized her hands. "My God, Wallis, wouldn't it be marvelous if I could play these bastards at their own game and beat them?"

She hadn't seen him so alive in years. "Oh, David," she said. "It could be so dangerous. I'm frightened."

"I'm not. To be perfectly honest, I think I'm rather beginning to enjoy this. The person I need now is Colonel da Cunha, so let's go and find him."

Five minutes later, in response to an urgent phone call to the lodge, Da Cunha hurried up to the house, where he found them waiting for him in the library.

"Your Royal Highness sent for me?"

"I did indeed, Colonel. Earlier today I asked if I could rely on your good offices. You were kind enough to say yes."

"If there is any way I can be of service, I will, sir."

"Then this is what I want you to do. Go and see the German Ambassador, Baron von Hoy-

ningen-Huene, now, this evening. Tell him I
wish to speak with General Schellenberg."

Da Cunha was unable to conceal his surprise.
"When would you wish this meeting to take
place?"

"Well, I rather thought it might be fun to
repeat, to a certain degree, his own exercise of
last night. You heard what Mr. Jackson and
Miss Winter had to say about events in the garden. I'll be having my usual cigar in the summerhouse. You could bring him to me. You
think he'll come?"

"I shouldn't think there would be much doubt
of it, sir."

"Another thing. I'd appreciate it if you could
get Mr. Jackson to repeat his role of last night.
A man of considerable resource. It would make
the Duchess feel rather easier in her mind to
know that he was watching my back. Do you
think he would do that for me?"

"Yes, sir. Would you wish me to be present?"

"Yes, but I think you might find the subject
matter of our conversation rather embarrassing. For your own sake, I suggest that you stand
a little way off."

Da Cunha hesitated. "Sir, forgive me for any
impertinence, but does this mean that you contemplate a move to Spain after all?"

"Now what would you think, Colonel?"

"Why, sir, I think you will sail on the *Excalibur* the day after tomorrow. It also occurs to me that Your Royal Highness is placing himself in a position of extreme danger. I only hope you are fully aware of the consequences of the course of action you contemplate, sir."

The Duke lit a cigarette, blew out a feathery trailer of smoke with that inimitable smile of his. "Difficult decisions, Colonel, are the privilege of rank."

When Schellenberg went into Huene's office it was really quite crowded. Fernandes da Cunha was by the window, looking out. There was the Ambassador himself, but the real surprise was Kleiber who stood at one side of the desk, his arm still in the sling. The look of pale triumph on his face should have warned Schellenberg to expect the worst.

"Colonel da Cunha is here on behalf of the Duke of Windsor," Huene said.

"Is this true?" Schellenberg said in astonishment, turning to Da Cunha.

"His Royal Highness would like to see you tonight. Secretly and informally. He's most anxious that his own people don't know anything about it."

"What does he suggest?"

"Roughly the same arrangement as pertained

last night. He'll be having a final cigar in the summerhouse at ten. If you leave your car down the hill and walk up on foot, I'll let you in by the side door. No one else in the villa need know anything about it."

"I can't believe it. At this stage in the game? Why?"

"Thirty-six hours only and the *Excalibur* sails," Da Cunha shrugged. "Perhaps this is the moment of truth for him."

"All right," Schellenberg said. "I'll be there."

"And I'll be with you," Kleiber said, his voice trembling with emotion.

It was a public confrontation which Schellenberg had not sought, but he had no intention of avoiding it. "I don't think so, not after this morning's debacle."

Huene said, "I'm sorry, General, but I have here a signal, received within the last hour from Reichsführer Himmler himself."

He held it out. Schellenberg said, "No, read it aloud, then we all know exactly where we stand."

> General Schellenberg will pursue his present task with the utmost vigor. Failure is unacceptable. At every possible opportunity he must—repeat must—avail himself of the assistance

of Sturmbannführer Kleiber. Any deviation from this order must be reported to me at once.

There was silence for a moment, then Schellenberg turned to Da Cunha with a smile. "So, Colonel, it would appear that when you open the door in the garden wall tonight, you open it to Sturmbannführer Kleiber also."

When Da Cunha was admitted to Jackson's office, the American was seated behind his desk dressed for work again in black tie and white tuxedo.

Da Cunha sniffed the air. "Chanel Number Five. Quite unmistakable. You can come out, senhorita. I've left my handcuffs at home."

He went to the sideboard and helped himself to a Scotch as she emerged from the washroom.

Jackson said, "What do you want?"

"I've got a job for you," Da Cunha told him. "Or rather, the Duke has. He's arranged to meet Schellenberg and Kleiber in the summerhouse. Same time as last night, and he'd like you to repeat your performance, Joe, up on the wall."

"You don't mean he intends to do a deal with them?" Hannah said. "He can't. It's not possible."

"Don't be silly, angel," Jackson told her. "If

that was his game, then why would he want me on hand?" He shook his head. "There's more to this than meets the eye—much more."

"You'll do as he asks?" Da Cunha said.

"Sure—I'll be there."

"Good." Da Cunha drained his glass. "An interesting night lies ahead, I feel. Let's hope we're all around in the morning to recall its events."

He went out and Hannah said, "I'm frightened, Joe, and I don't understand it. Not any of it. What can the Duke be thinking of?"

Jackson went and poured himself a drink. "Perhaps he's started to fight back."

FOURTEEN

JACKSON was on the wall again just after nine-thirty, dressed, as he had been the previous night, in black, the Browning ready in his hand. It was not very comfortable, but at least it wasn't raining.

After a while, Da Cunha appeared, walking along the path through the shrubbery. He checked the door, then waited. A little later, the Duke appeared. He wore evening dress, and a light tweed coat hung from his shoulders as a protection against the night air, which was rather chilly.

He moved closer to the summerhouse. "Are you there, Mr. Jackson?" he asked in a low voice.

"Yes, sir," Jackson replied.

The Duke took a Havana cigar from a leather case and lit it, still standing there in the path. At the same moment Jackson heard footsteps approaching in the road outside. There was a tap at the door, Da Cunha opened it, and Schellenberg entered followed by Kleiber.

"General Schellenberg and Sturmbannführer Kleiber," Da Cunha made the introductions and withdrew to a discreet distance.

"Ah, the gentleman who was waiting for me at Rosario this morning?" the Duke said.

"An unfortunate error, Your Royal Highness," Schellenberg told him.

"An unnecessary one. Especially if you'd made an honest, direct approach to me in the first place. Suggestions, General, veiled hints, that's all I've had. What exactly is it that your government is offering?"

"It is well known, sir, that the post of Governor of the Bahamas has few attractions for you. In the circumstances, you would perhaps prefer to stay on in Europe. In Spain, for example, or Switzerland. I am authorized to say that if, because of circumstances, you find yourself in financial difficulties by making such a move, a sum of fifty million Swiss francs could be made available on deposit in Geneva."

"Nonsense, General Schellenberg. Sheer

bloody, unadulterated nonsense. The Führer doesn't want me in Spain or Switzerland. He wants me in Germany, to be on hand for the day the German army enters London. A familiar face to give the British people confidence. Is this not so?"

"What can I say, sir?"

"My boat sails the day after tomorrow and I don't want to go. I admit that. The British Government have treated me badly—damn badly— and if my services matter so little to them..." He shrugged. "Thirty-six hours, that's all I've got, but if I'm to throw myself into the game on your side, I must know exactly what I'm getting into."

Kleiber started to speak and Schellenberg cut him short. "May I ask Your Royal Highness a direct question? If necessary, would you be prepared to ascend the throne again?"

"Certainly," the Duke said. "I would naturally expect the Duchess to be accepted as my consort."

"I foresee no difficulty there, sir."

"Naturally, if I am to take so drastic a step, an action which, to put it mildly, would cause something of a stir in the world, I shall require some evidence of cooperation on the part of the Führer."

"And what would satisfy Your Royal Highness?"

"If the Duchess and I are to make plans to return to England, we must know by what date the Führer thinks we should be ready to depart."

Schellenberg saw it all then, or thought he did, but contented himself with saying, "Very well, sir. I understand your interest in the timing involved. I will convey this to Reichsminister von Ribbentrop, who will no doubt communicate it to the Führer without delay."

"At once, General," the Duke said. "You have only tomorrow. It would distress me to leave on the *Excalibur*, but I will go if I must. Any communication you have for me, put through Colonel da Cunha. There must be no question of the British Embassy getting even a hint of our negotiations."

"Of course, sir," Schellenberg said. "I'll be in touch at the earliest possible moment. The instant I obtain a reply from Berlin. And now, goodnight to you."

He moved to the gate followed by Kleiber; Da Cunha opened it for them and locked it after they had passed through. Jackson, on the wall, made no move until the sound of their footsteps had faded down the hill.

"Mr. Jackson?"

"Yes, sir." The American dropped down into the shrubbery and approached the summer-house.

"Did you hear that?"

"I think I got most of it."

"Well, what do you think? Will they play ball, isn't that the American phrase?"

"I'd say that depends on how badly they need you, sir."

"If they occupy England, very badly indeed. Still, thank you for coming." The Duke held out his hand. "May I count on you again? For obvious reasons, it would be unwise for me to approach our own intelligence people at the moment."

"Yes, sir."

"Excellent. I'll say good night then. Colonel da Cunha will let you out."

He walked away through the shrubbery and Da Cunha approached. "Did you hear any of it?" Jackson asked him.

"No, and I don't want to. Now get out of here and quickly. I should have changed the gate guard twenty minutes ago."

"He's lying," Schellenberg said. "I don't believe a word of it."

They were in Huene's office again. The Am-

bassador sat behind his desk, and Kleiber stood
at the other end facing Schellenberg.

"I was there too, remember, and I believed
him. Why not? They threw him out on his ear,
didn't they? Now we're giving him a chance to
go back in style, regain his throne, and with the
woman he loves at his side. That's all he really
wants."

Huene shook his head. "I don't agree. We'll
be landing in Britain in a matter of weeks, the
whole world knows that. As I see it, the Duke
is just being practical. A timetable isn't an un-
reasonable request. And if he gives his word . . ."

"I know," Schellenberg said. "A man of finest
honor. But it occurs to me that there may come
a time for any man when he's at his most honorable by acting dishonorably for the sake of a
cause he believes in."

"We're going around in circles," Kleiber said.
"Are you going to get in touch with Reichsminister von Ribbentrop or must I do it for you?"

"No," Schellenberg said. "That won't be necessary. I'll get a signal off right away. I'll leave
you to impart the glad tidings to Reichsführer
Himmler. You'll enjoy doing that."

Himmler often spent the night in a small
room adjacent to his office at Prinz Albrechtstrasse. Kleiber's rather lengthy signal had

been routed through the Madrid Embassy and
had been delayed because of technical difficulties on the line. It was ten-thirty on the following morning before it arrived on his desk.

He read it through, lips pursed, then sat
there, staring into space, thinking about it. Finally, he put the signal to one side and started
to work his way through his correspondence,
waiting for Von Ribbentrop to make the first
move.

It was just after eleven when the phone rang.
The Reichsminister said, "I've had a signal from
Schellenberg. Rather remarkable. Frankly, I'm
not sure what to do about it. I wondered whether
the Führer..."

"No," Himmler said firmly. "The Führer is
particularly busy at the moment, as you well
know. There are some burdens we must carry
for him. I, too, have received a signal from Lisbon. I know that the Führer has placed the
Windsor affair in your lap particularly, but if
you thought it helpful, I would be happy to discuss it with you."

"I'll be there in fifteen minutes," Von Ribbentrop said and hung up.

It was just after noon when Walter Monckton
was shown into the library, where he was
greeted with real affection by both the Duke
and Duchess. It had been Monckton who, more

than anyone else, had provided not only guidance but friendship during the dark days of the Abdication Crisis.

"I suppose Winston's sent you to make sure I get on that damn boat tomorrow?" the Duke said.

"Well, sir, the Prime Minister and indeed His Majesty, have been concerned at the delays in the matter. I know, sir, that this Bahamas appointment is not to your liking, but there are certain advantages."

"Name one, Walter," the Duchess suggested.

Monckton smiled amiably. "The climate? No, sir, there have been rumors of an unhealthy German interest in your presence here."

"Walter, you're behind the times. It's our own Secret Service I have to worry about, according to Madrid gossip."

"But that's absurd, sir. You can't possibly believe such a thing."

"Do you know the Marqués de Estella, Primo de Rivera? An old friend, Walter, very highly connected with the Spanish government. He has assured me on several occasions that there is considerable substance to these rumors."

"But what would be the object, sir? I don't understand."

"Well, if there was any kind of possibility that I was going to refuse to go to the Bahamas, the idea seems to be that they'd take me by force. De Rivera is coming for lunch today. You'd be doing me a favor if you'd talk to him about this thing. Hear his evidence."

"You've no idea what it's been like here, Walter," the Duchess told him. "Anonymous letters—even phone calls. We can't take a step without falling over a policeman."

"Now, Wallis," the Duke took her hands in his. "You worry too much. Go and get ready for lunch. He'll be here soon."

When she had gone, he went to the sideboard and poured himself a large Scotch. Monckton said, "Good Lord, sir, in all the time I've known you I've never seen you take a drink before seven in the evening."

"I know, Walter, but I need it today. By God, I really do need it. Tell me, old friend, since we first knew each other at Oxford, have I ever been less than honest with you?"

"No, sir."

"Then I ask you to trust me now. Walter, when the *Excalibur* sails tomorrow, I shall be on board, I promise you, but for the moment, it's essential that certain people still get the impression that I'm vacillating. Will you spend the rest of the day with De Rivera for me? Tell him how shocked you are at my fears. That I'm

threatening not to leave on the boat. Ask him
for proof of these plots he speaks of."

Monckton said gravely, "And am I not to be
permitted to know what's really going on, sir?"

"No, Walter. Not for the moment."

Monckton sighed. "Very well. I'll do what I
can."

"Good—excellent," the Duke said.

There was a knock at the door, and a footman
appeared. "The Marqués de Estella is here,
Your Royal Highness," he said and Primo de
Rivera entered.

Himmler said, "If we give him our time schedule, what exactly is it that we're giving away?"

"You mean show him the entire plan?" Von
Ribbentrop said in horror.

Himmler gave one of his rare smiles. "The
whole thing is quite academic. Look at it this
way. A few weeks ago, the British Army left
most of its equipment on the beaches at Dunkirk. Their Home Guard drill with pikes and
pitchforks. They have less than two hundred
tanks. They are desperately short of fighter
planes." Himmler paused for a moment. "Con-
ditions for a landing are at their most favorable
in the period between September the nineteenth to the twenty-sixth. Anyone with a
Channel map and a tide schedule knows that.

The Luftwaffe will have crushed all opposition in the air by then, and without air support the Royal Navy is most effectively neutralized. No, if Winston Churchill had the entire plan of Sea Lion in his hands at this very moment, he has neither the resources nor the capability to stop it."

"So, you think we should meet the Duke's demand."

"My dear Von Ribbentrop, it is you to whom the Führer entrusted the Windsor affair, in the confident expectation of a successful conclusion. I, of course, can only advise you, but I must say that I don't see how you can go far wrong under the circumstances."

It was just after five o'clock when the signal was received at the Legation, and Huene sent for Schellenberg and Kleiber at once.

"From Reichsminister von Ribbentrop. It simply says: 'Demands acceptable. Details requested follow.'"

Kleiber turned to Schellenberg, his eyes ablaze with triumph. "So, you see, General, I knew my man. Better than you did, I knew my man. I'll go to the communications room and wait for the signal to come through."

When the door had closed behind him, Schellenberg lit a cigarette and laughed out loud.

"This isn't just Ribbentrop, you realize that? It's Himmler as well. A champagne saleman and a chicken farmer. That is really an unbeatable combination, you must admit."

"General Schellenberg," Huene said. "I can listen to no more of this. I have a family to consider. Relatives back home."

"Of course," Schellenberg said. "Stupid of me to allow emotion to take over. The trouble is that one remembers occasionally that one is a human being and not just a zombie walking through the canebrake. I detest stupidity."

The door opened and Kleiber entered with a sealed envelope. "They put it through the encoder, General, so that even the coding clerk didn't see it. It was marked for your eyes only."

Schellenberg weighed the envelope in his hands. "And for the Duke of Windsor's also, I presume?"

"Shall I get hold of Da Cunha?" Huene asked.

Schellenberg nodded. "Better tell him to arrange another meeting with the Duke. The same time and place as last night will do."

He slipped the envelope into his inside pocket. Kleiber went out, and Schellenberg followed. At the door, he paused and turned to Huene. "I leave you with one happy thought. I think we've just lost the war."

*   *   *

Walter Monckton heaved a sigh of relief as Primo de Rivera was shown to his car. He stood on the steps beside the Duke, waving cheerfully.

"I really must protest, sir. I don't think I've ever heard such nonsense in my life as I've taken from that gentleman tonight. I asked him for some sort of documentary evidence, and he can show me nothing. He then had the infernal cheek to inform me that within ten days he'll have all the evidence we'll need."

"And asked you to postpone any sailing tomorrow? Poor Walter. You've earned a drink, and I really am most grateful."

As they went in, Monckton said, "And now, sir, may I be permitted to know the object of the exercise?"

"Perhaps tomorrow," the Duke said as they went into the drawing room, where the Duchess was sitting by the fire with Dr. Ricardo de Espirito Santo é Silva and his wife. "Now, who's for a drink?"

There was a discreet knock at the door, and a footman came in. "Colonel da Cunha to see Your Royal Highness."

"Do please excuse me, everyone. Security arrangements for tomorrow. See to the drinks, there's a good chap, Walter."

He sat in the summerhouse, a coat around

his shoulders, and examined the documents the envelope contained, by the light of a small flashlight. Schellenberg and Kleiber waited by the door.

"Very interesting," the Duke said finally. "Quite brilliant. I can't fault it."

He put the two sheets of paper back into the envelope, and Schellenberg said, "You are satisfied then, sir?"

"Yes."

"And the sailing tomorrow?"

"Simply can't take place. The Duchess isn't at all well. I should think we'll have to get the doctor first thing in the morning. The *Excalibur* leaves at noon. After she's gone, we can make other arrangements."

"Of course, sir."

"Good, then I'll say good night, gentlemen."

Da Cunha, who was standing by the gate, let them out. Joe Jackson, on the wall, waited, then dropped to the ground.

The Duke took the envelope from his pocket. "You'd never believe what's in there, Mr. Jackson."

"I could hazard a guess, sir."

"Wait here for me, in the summerhouse. I'll be back as quickly as I can with something of supreme importance, I assure you."

"Very well, sir."

The Duke turned to Da Cunha. "If you'd keep him company, Colonel, I'd really be most grateful."

He hurried away along the path.

The Duchess found him in the library, the two signal sheets open on the desk before him.

"What are the others doing?"

"Playing cards. What have you got there?"

"The most astonishing thing you ever read in your life, Wallis. Operation Sea Lion—the German plan for the invasion of England, supplied by Von Ribbentrop in the fond hope that it might make me see which side my bread is buttered on."

She locked the door and came back to the desk. "Look at this," he said. "Eagle Day, August the thirteenth. The Luftwaffe launches a devastating strike on the airfields of the south of England aimed at destroying the RAF."

"And the invasion?" she said.

"Must take place between the nineteenth and the twenty-sixth of September. A question of the kind of moon and tide times. After that, it's no good because they'll be into the autumn and much more unpredictable weather. Imagine a thousand barges halfway across the Channel and a force-eight gale springing up."

"But what does it all mean?" she said. "Can anything be done about it?"

"Yes, I think something can. The whole thing hinges on air superiority. As long as the RAF still functions, the Royal Navy commands the Channel and no invasion can possibly succeed. But here on sheet two, Directive 17. The Luftwaffe have orders to eliminate the RAF as a first priority. Goering says here that he estimates accomplishing this in two weeks."

"My God."

"Which brings us to the flaw in the whole plan," the Duke told her. "The contingency section. If for any reason the Luftwaffe have not succeeded in crushing the RAF by the seventeenth of September, then Operation Sea Lion will be canceled. The plan is quite specific on that point."

"And what happens then?"

"He'll turn on Russia, and that, my love, will be the end of him. I'm sure I saw a typewriter in the cupboard over there the other day. Not that I'm any expert, but two fingers should suffice."

"For what, David?"

"To make a copy of this little lot, Wallis. For Mr. Jackson."

* * *

It was forty minutes before he was back at the summerhouse where Jackson and Da Cunha still waited.

"So very sorry, Mr. Jackson, but I had to copy what was in the envelope Schellenberg gave me, and my typing isn't what it should be."

"That's all right, sir."

The Duke gave him the envelope. "What that contains is of supreme importance to the British Government at this time. I've addressed it to Mr. Winston Churchill and marked it for his eyes alone. After I've sailed tomorrow, I'd be obliged if you would pass it to Sir Walford Selby at the British Embassy with my compliments. The original, I shall give to my good friend Walter Monckton to pass on to Mr. Churchill personally when he returns to London."

"A case of hedging your bets, sir?"

"Accidents do happen. You know, Mr. Jackson, once, in France during the First World War, I got out of my staff car and walked forward to view a trench. A few minutes later, the car was riddled with machine gun bullets, killing the driver. I've often wondered, over the years, why I was spared on that occasion. I've never looked upon myself as a religious man, but perhaps tonight provides some sort of answer."

"Sir, it's been a privilege to know you."

"And you, Mr. Jackson."

The Duke shook his hand. Da Cunha opened the door and showed him out. As he locked it, the Duke said, "Not long now, Colonel, and you'll be rid of me."

"A new world, sir, new plans. Something to look forward to."

"Yes, of course," the Duke said. "Surf beating on the shore, palm trees swaying, and three thousand miles away from the war. Who could ask for more? Good night to you, Colonel da Cunha," and he walked away quickly.

When Joe Jackson went up the back stairs to the apartment an hour later, Hannah was waiting anxiously.

She felt his sweater. "My God, you're wet through. Joe, I was so worried. What happened?"

He put the envelope the Duke had given him on the table and sat down wearily.

"Nothing much," he said. "I just had to hang around, waiting for a while for a very remarkable man."

FIFTEEN

WALTER MONCKTON and Dr. Ricardo de Espirito Santo é Silva waited in the library. It was almost ten o'clock and Monckton paced up and down anxiously. The door opened, and the Duke entered, his face grave.

"Well, sir?" Monckton asked. "How is she?"

"Not too good, I'm afraid. Some sort of virus, the doctor thinks. There can certainly be no question of her traveling, not until we've fully sorted out what the problem is."

"But sir, *Excalibur* leaves in two hours. We cannot possibly delay its sailing. Your luggage is already on board."

"There will be other boats, Walter. A delay of a few days, a week or two, even, is not going to matter one way or the other." He turned to Santo é Silva. "I really must apologize for this last-minute contretemps, Doctor. We've imposed enough on your generosity as it is."

"Your Royal Highness, I am entirely at your disposal, as always. My house is yours for as long as need be. If you will excuse me now, I will go and make sure that the household staff are made aware of the change of plan."

As the door closed behind him, Monckton said, "Really, sir, I must ask you to think again. Is the Duchess so ill that an ocean voyage wouldn't prove beneficial?"

"To tell you the truth, Walter, she's as fit as a fiddle." The Duke took him by the arm and led him out to the terrace.

"But I don't understand."

"You will, Walter, but tell me. Is Da Cunha on hand?"

"No, sir, he's at the docks. I didn't wish to alarm you, but police headquarters had an anonymous phone call saying there was a bomb on board *Excalibur.* The work of some crank perhaps. He told me they were searching the ship from stem to stern. Look, what is going on, sir?"

The Duke leaned on the balustrade with both hands. "Walter, I reminded you yesterday that we'd always been completely honest with each other."

"Yes, sir?"

"Well, I'm afraid that's no longer true. I had a meeting with Schellenberg here in the garden last night."

"Good God."

"Yes, Walter, they think I'm on their side now. That I'm not going to the Bahamas after all. In return, I gain this." He took the buff envelope from his inside pocket. "A present for Winston," he smiled. "With my love, of course."

Monckton held the envelope in both hands, a slightly dazed look in his eyes. "But what happens now, sir? What are your intentions?"

"To sail on the *Excalibur*. Now this is what you do. Tell our esteemed host you're going down to the docks to inform Colonel da Cunha we won't be sailing and to retrieve the luggage. Oh, and take Mrs. Fryth, the new maid, with you. That will seem normal enough."

"Then what?"

"Return here at precisely eleven-thirty. The moment you arrive, Wallis and I will join you, and we'll make a dash for the ship. If the timing is right, we should arrive just as they're taking up the gangplank."

"And you wish me to inform Colonel da Cunha of this plan?"

"Yes—most certainly." The Duke smiled. "We're into the home stretch, Walter, three lengths clear of the field. We'll beat them, you'll see."

When he went into the bedroom, the shades were drawn and the room was in half-darkness.

"Wallis?" he whispered and sat on the edge of the bed.

"David, is anything wrong?" She pushed herself up against the pillows.

"Not a thing, my darling, we're exactly on course. I thought your performance with the doctor was perfection itself. I'm sure that by now the news has reached the German Legation that we're not leaving. In other words, that I'm doing exactly as promised."

"And what happens now?"

He took one of her hands in his and explained quickly.

Schellenberg had slept late for once. It was almost ten-thirty when the phone rang at the side of the bed.

"Huene here."

"Good morning," Schellenberg said. "How are things?"

"We had a report that a car turned up at the

docks half an hour ago with all their luggage. It was loaded on board immediately."

"Good God!" Schellenberg pushed himself up on one elbow.

"No need to panic. I've just heard from the house that the Duchess is unwell. The doctor's confined her to bed. They definitely won't be sailing." There was a silence. "Are you still there, General? Will you be coming in?"

"Yes, I suppose so," Schellenberg said. "There's the next move to work out now, isn't there? When to get them out and how."

He put down the phone, lit a cigarette, and leaned back against the pillow. Strange, but he felt curiously disappointed.

Just before eleven-thirty, the Duke was waiting at the bedroom window, the Duchess at his shoulder, fully dressed.

"Come on, Walter," the Duke whispered, glancing at his watch again. "Don't let me down now."

A moment later, the Buick came up the drive and braked to a halt at the front door. Walter Monckton got out and looked up at the bedroom window.

"Here we go, Wallis." The Duke took her by the arm. "Don't stop for anything."

They hurried down the stairs, and a surprised

footman ran to open the front door for them. At that moment, Santo é Silva came out of the library. He paused, a look of astonishment on his face.

"But Your Royal Highness..."

"So awfully kind of you to have put up with us for so long. Sincerely regret the inconvenience," the Duke said and kept on moving.

"But Her Grace..."

"Is feeling much better now. Sea air will do her a world of good."

They were into the rear of the Buick in an instant. Monckton followed, slamming the door, and called to the driver. The wheels spun, churning the gravel, and they were away.

Dr. Ricardo de Espirito Santo é Silva turned, hurried into the library, and picked up the telephone.

When Kleiber went into Huene's office, he found the Ambassador pacing up and down, obviously very agitated indeed.

"Ambassador. You sent for me?"

"I've tried to get hold of General Schellenberg, but it seems he's already left his hotel. Bad news, I'm afraid. I've just heard from the villa that the Duke and Duchess left in a considerable hurry for the *Excalibur* some ten or fifteen minutes ago. He's tricked us. He's sailing for the Bahamas after all."

"But he can't do that." Kleiber was very pale. "He gave his word, made a bargain. We kept our part."

Huene said, "A disastrous situation, but there's nothing any of us can do about it."

Kleiber turned, tight-lipped, and went out. Sindermann was waiting outside and could tell at once from Kleiber's face that something was seriously wrong.

"Sturmbannführer?"

"The Duke," Kleiber said grimly. "He's sold us out. They're sailing on the *Excalibur* after all."

"So—we've lost, Sturmbannführer? He must be laughing all over his face."

"I'm sure he is, Gunter, so let's make sure he dies laughing, shall we? You go downstairs and get the car started. I'll be with you in a few minutes."

"And General Schellenberg?"

"To hell with General Schellenberg."

He burst into the armory and the startled sergeant in charge leaped to attention.

"Sturmbannführer. May I help you?"

"I want a rifle." Kleiber went around behind

the counter. "Any decent rifle will do. What's this, for instance?"

"A new development by Walther. Semiautomatic."

"Is it loaded?"

The sergeant opened a cupboard, revealing an assortment of magazines, took one out, and rammed it into place.

"It is now. Ten-round, staggered-row. box magazine. A really excellent combat weapon and astonishingly accurate on rapid fire at up to a thousand yards."

"Good, I'll take it." Kleiber made for the door.

"Please, Sturmbannführer," the sergeant called. "You must sign for it."

But Kleiber was already gone. The sergeant started toward the door, paused, then went back to the counter. He picked up the internal telephone and asked to be put through to the Ambassador.

As Schellenberg's Buick entered the gates of the Legation, Zeidler had to wrench the wheel sharply to one side as a black Mercedes sedan hurtled toward them. Schellenberg had a brief glimpse of Sindermann at the wheel, Kleiber beside him, and then they were gone.

"A close thing, General," Zeidler said as he pulled in at the bottom of the steps leading up to the entrance. "I wonder where they were going in such a hurry?"

"So do I," Schellenberg said.

As he got out of the car, Huene appeared on the porch. "General Schellenberg. Thank heavens you're here."

"What's happened?" Schellenberg demanded.

"The Duke," Huene said, "is leaving on the *Excalibur*. He's fooled us. Fooled us all."

"And where was Kleiber going in such a hurry?"

"I've just been informed he's drawn a rifle from the armory."

Walter Schellenberg turned and ran down the steps to the car. "The Alcantara Docks," he told Zeidler. "The pier the *Excalibur* is leaving from, and drive like you've never done before!"

The entrance to the docks was heavily guarded, so much was obvious. All vehicles were being closely inspected as they entered. As the Mercedes coasted past, Kleiber noticed Da Cunha standing by the gate. The gangplank had already been pulled in and lines were being cast off.

"What are you going to do, Sturmbannführer?" Sindermann asked. "We'll never get past the gate and soon it will be too late."

"I've just had a thought, Gunter. Wasn't that

the American's bar we passed a couple of minutes ago?"

"Yes, Sturmbannführer."

"Then let's see if he's at home. He could be
the solution to all our problems."

Joe Jackson and Hannah were standing on
the wooden balcony of the apartment above the
club, looking upriver toward the Alcantara
Docks and the *Excalibur*, whose funnels tow-
ered above a jumble of dock buildings.

"We'll get a much better view when the tugs
have pulled her out into midstream," Jackson
told her.

The door of the living room was flung open,
and as they turned Kleiber and Sindermann
entered, both holding Walther automatics.

Kleiber said, "What I say, I will say only once,
Herr Jackson."

Jackson had an arm around Hannah's shoulder. "Okay, get on with it."

"I desire to gain entrance to the Alcantara
Docks, but unfortunately the gate is very heavily guarded by Security Police."

"So?"

"Colonel da Cunha is on duty there personally. It occurs to me that he will allow you to
pass through the gate on the excuse that you
wish to watch the *Excalibur* leave. Only natural

after your part in the affair. I shall be under the canvas cover of the bucket seat of your Mercedes sports car, crouched behind you. Now, I could say that I'll blow your spine out if you attempt to give me away at the gate, but there's no need. Sindermann will be here with Fräulein Winter in his charge. You follow me?"

Sindermann grabbed her by the hair and rammed the muzzle of his Walther under her chin.

"Five seconds," Kleiber said. "That's all you have to make up your mind."

"Okay." Jackson raised his hands defensively. "We play it your way. What do you want me to do?"

As the Buick neared the docks, Joe Jackson's bar coming up on their left, Zeidler braked suddenly so that Schellenberg was thrown forward.

"See, General?" He pointed at the black Mercedes parked at the end of the wharf. "It's them. I know the car. It has the Embassy plates on it."

"Pull over behind it," Schellenberg told him.

There was no sign of life in the car, but when he tried the side door of the club it opened to his touch. He paused for a moment, then went upstairs cautiously, his hands in his pockets.

Sindermann sat on one side of the table, Hannah on the other. She reached for the coffee pot.

"Careful," he warned her.

"I only want a cup of coffee," she said, then hurled the scalding contents of the pot into his face and started for the door. As he cried out in anguish, she tripped over one of the oriental rugs and fell. A second later, he had her by the hair, jerking her to her feet.

"Now then, you bitch, I'll make you pay."

"I don't think so," Schellenberg said softly.

He was standing just inside the door, the Mauser with the bulbous silencer in his right hand. Sindermann slipped behind her, ramming the Walther into her side.

"Drop it," he ordered. "Now—or she dies."

Schellenberg's arm swung up and he shot him through the head instantly. The top of Sindermann's skull fragmented and the force of the bullet sent him back out across the balcony and over the rail into the river below.

Hannah had fallen to one knee, blood across her hair and face. As he helped her to her feet, Schellenberg said urgently, "Kleiber? Where is he?"

"The docks," she said. "He forced Joe to take him there, hidden in the back of the sports car."

He took her hand, turned, and hurried down the stairs.

As the Buick swerved in at the gate, several soldiers ran forward to block its way. Colonel da Cunha was standing in the entrance of the gatehouse, talking to Walter Monckton. He came over at once, frowning at the sight of Hannah Winter, who sat beside Schellenberg, blood on her face.

"What's happened? Explain yourself, General."

"Has Joe come through in the silver sports car?" Hannah demanded.

"Why yes, several minutes ago. He told me he wished to catch a last glimpse of the Duke."

"Kleiber was with him," Schellenberg said. "Hidden in the back, and he has a rifle."

Walter Monckton, who had appeared behind Da Cunha, said in horror, "Good God, what can we do?"

There was a sudden cheer. As they turned, the Duke and Duchess appeared on the upper deck and waved to the dock workers below.

Monckton ran forward, shouting frantically. "Go back, David! For God's sake, go back!"

The Duke and Duchess, unable to hear a thing he was saying, waved, smiling.

It was Hannah then who, looking wildly

about her, saw the silver Mercedes parked outside the warehouse a hundred yards away.

"There!" she cried, pointing. "Joe's car."

As Zeidler gunned the motor, Da Cunha
jumped on the running board and the car surged
forward, a dozen or fifteen armed police running
behind.

The sports car was parked beside a green door
marked *Fire Exit*. Schellenberg flung it open
and found stone steps ascending into darkness.
He pulled out his Mauser and went up on the
run.

Willi Kleiber stood behind Jackson at the
parapet. The *Excalibur* was even farther out
into the stream now. As she sounded her whistle, the Duke and Duchess entered a railed-off
enclosure in the stern that had obviously been
specially set aside for them.

"Beautiful," Kleiber said. "I can get two for
the price of one."

"Don't be a fool, man," Jackson told him.
"There's nothing to be gained now."

"He made fools of us—all of us," Kleiber answered. "The Führer himself, even. Now, he
pays."

He rammed the butt of the Walther into Jackson's side. The American went down with a

groan and Kleiber knelt, resting the Walther on the parapet, taking careful aim at the Duke.

As he squeezed the trigger, Jackson, half unconscious as he was, grappled with him. The ship's whistle roared again at that moment, drowning the sound of the shot, and the bullet plowed into the deck several feet to one side of the Duke and Duchess, who were totally unaware of the fact in the noise and confusion of their departure.

Kleiber kicked out at Jackson, pushing him away, and took aim for the second time. The door to the stairs behind burst open, a familiar voice cried, "Kleiber!"

Kleiber turned, hate taking complete possession of him now, the rifle coming up, and Schellenberg shot him in the right shoulder, the heavy bullet turning him in a circle. The next two shattered his spine, driving him against the parapet, the rifle flying into space.

Colonel da Cunha knelt down beside him, but no examination was necessary. He glanced up. "You are a difficult man to understand, General Schellenberg."

"Something I live with every day of my life."

"You will be going home soon, I trust, back to Berlin?"

"Today, if I can manage it."

"Good," Da Cunha mopped sweat from his

face with a handkerchief. "One episode like this is enough in any policeman's career."

Hannah arrived and dropped to one knee beside Jackson, who was trying to sit up.

"Did he make it?"

"Yes," she said. "Thanks to General Schellenberg."

Schellenberg pocketed his Mauser, turned, and moved toward the door. As he started down the stairs, she caught up with him, grabbing him by the sleeve.

"You're going back to Berlin, aren't you?"

"Yes."

"Why?"

"Because I have no choice, and I think, in your heart, you know this. For me, it is too late."

He started down the stairs again. She called, "Walter!" and there was desperation in her voice, a kind of rage at life and the cruelty of it.

"Did I ever tell you that when you sing, you sound like Billie Holiday on one of her better days?" he said.

His footsteps echoed hollowly for a while as he descended, the door banged, and he was gone.

As the *Excalibur* moved out to sea from the mouth of the Tagus, the Duchess went in search of the Duke and found him still standing in the stern.

"I've brought you a scarf," she said.

"Why, thank you, Wallis."

She took his arm and they stood there at the rail together. "It could be worse, David, the Bahamas, I mean. We'll make it work, you'll see, so try not to be too disappointed. After all, we have each other."

"Of course we do, and I'm not the slightest bit disappointed." He smiled that wonderful smile that illuminated not only himself, but everything about him. "In fact, to be perfectly honest, Wallis, I feel rather pleased with myself."

"But will anyone ever know, David?" she said.

"I will, my love." He kissed her gently on the brow. "And so will you. That's all that matters."

When Schellenberg entered his office at Prinz Albrechtstrasse at three o'clock the following afternoon, he had been traveling for just over twenty-four hours with only the occasional nap to keep him going. His tweed suit was crumpled and he badly needed a shave.

He had been in the room for only a couple of minutes when the door was opened without ceremony and Heydrich entered.

"You look as if you haven't slept for a week."

"I only feel that way."

"He knows you're here, Walter. Wants you upstairs right away. What a mess this thing turned out to be, but I'm sorry. I can't help you now. This time, you're finished."

"Oh, I don't know," Schellenberg said. "Let's wait and see, shall we?"

He delivered his report, standing in front of Himmler's desk, holding nothing back of any consequence.

When he had finished, there was silence for a moment, then Himmler said, "You were right to execute Kleiber as you did. He was a fool. There was nothing to be gained from assassinating the Duke at that stage in the affair."

Schellenberg said, "There is, of course, the question of the information passed on to the Duke. . . ."

"By order of Von Ribbentrop." Himmler sighed. "Yes, I do feel the Reichsminister has been a little injudicious in that respect."

"Will you inform the Führer?"

"On another occasion, perhaps. One that is more suited to my purposes."

Which boded ill for Ribbentrop.

Schellenberg said, "And the details of Sea Lion, Reichsführer? What can we do about that?

The Duke will certainly have passed them on to the Prime Minister, probably using Walter Monckton as his messenger."

"But to what avail? There are only two periods before the autumn gales when the tide is right for a landing. The British know that as well as we do. The important point is that there will be nothing they can do about it. In the same way, the fact that they now know the date of Eagle Day makes little difference when they're hardly in a position to defend themselves against the might of the Luftwaffe."

"But Reichsführer, they will also know now, that if Goering fails in his task, if they can hold until the seventeenth of September, Operation Sea Lion will be aborted and the Führer will turn his attention East."

Himmler said, "Are you seriously suggesting that the mightiest air force the world has ever seen, a force that has taken total control of the skies of Europe, can be held back by a handful of Spitfire pilots with virtually no combat experience?"

"Yes, Reichsführer, put that way, I suppose it does sound rather absurd."

"You're tired, General. You've been through a great deal. I suggest you go home now. Take a week off, and when you return you'll see things in perspective again."

"Thank you, Reichsführer."

Schellenberg went out, closing the door softly behind him, and walked through the anteroom.

He said softly, "Am I really the only sane man in a world gone mad?"

EPILOGUE

HANNAH WINTER returned to America a month later on the same boat as Connie Jones and the boys. Joe Jackson stayed in Lisbon until October, but news of the Battle of Britain proved too much for him and he sold the club, took passage to England on a Portuguese boat, and joined the RAF.

By April, 1942, he was a squadron leader with a D.S.O. and two D.F.C.s to his name. On the fifth of April, he was reported missing, believed killed, having been last seen pursuing two ME-109's across the Channel. Perhaps, for once, he had failed to watch the sun.

Hannah worked with the USO for some time and finally returned to England at the begin-

ning of 1944 to tour American Air Force bases.
During the spring of that year, the Luftwaffe
renewed its night attacks against London in
what became known as the Little Blitz, and
Hannah Winter, along with forty-two other people, was killed instantly when a club on Curzon
Street, at which she was appearing, received a
direct hit.

Heydrich was assassinated in Prague in
June, 1942, by a team of Czech agents specially
recruited for the job. By way of reprisal, the
Nazis destroyed the village of Lidice and mur-
dered the entire adult population.

Himmler, captured by British Forces after
the war, took poison when his identity was discovered.

Walter Schellenberg became Head of the
Combined Secret Services in 1944, playing out
the farce to the end, surviving all of them. In
1945, he was imprisoned at Landsberg and tes-
tified at various war crime trials before being
tried himself on the charge of having been a
member of an illegal organization, the SS.

He was sentenced to six years and perhaps
because, for an officer with his background,
there had been a surprising number of wit-
nesses who had spoken in his favor at his trial,
he was released after only two years' impris-
onment, in 1951. He died of cancer at the age

of forty-two and is buried in the public cemetery at Turin.

The Duke of Windsor, posted as far away from the war as possible, first as Governor of the Bahamas, then of Bermuda, had already made his contribution: probably one of the most important of the entire war.

At the height of the Battle of Britain on September 15, 1940, Winston Churchill visited Air Vice Marshal Keith Park at Number 2 Group's operation room at Uxbridge.

With the strongest concentration of planes the Luftwaffe had ever sent over, the RAF were stretched to breaking point. The Prime Minister asked what reserves there were to bring in.

"None, sir," Park told him. "Everything's up there."

"Hold on," the Prime Minister told him. "Two more days, that's all and it will be over."

Park looked at him in amazement. "But how can you be sure, Prime Minister? Is this information from a trustworthy source?"

Winston Churchill smiled. "I have it on the most impeccable authority," he said.